MUFFLED

ALSO BY JENNIFER GENNARI

My Mixed-Up Berry Blue Summer

MUFFLED

Jennifer Gennari

Simon & Schuster Books for Young Readers
NEW YORK   LONDON   TORONTO   SYDNEY   NEW DELHI

SIMON & SCHUSTER BOOKS FOR YOUNG READERS
An imprint of Simon & Schuster Children's Publishing Division
1230 Avenue of the Americas, New York, New York 10020

This book is a work of fiction. Any references to historical events, real people, or real places are used fictitiously. Other names, characters, places, and events are products of the author's imagination, and any resemblance to actual events or places or persons, living or dead, is entirely coincidental.

For information about special discounts for bulk purchases, please contact
Simon & Schuster Special Sales at 1-866-506-1949 or business@simonandschuster.com.
The Simon & Schuster Speakers Bureau can bring authors to your live event.
For more information or to book an event, contact the Simon & Schuster Speakers
Bureau at 1-866-248-3049 or visit our website at www.simonspeakers.com.
Also available in a Simon & Schuster Books for Young Readers hardcover edition
Interior design by Hilary Zarycky
The text for this book was set in New Baskerville.
Manufactured in the United States of America
0921 OFF
First Simon & Schuster Books for Young Readers paperback edition October 2021
2 4 6 8 10 9 7 5 3 1
The Library of Congress has cataloged the hardcover edition as follows:
Names: Gennari, Jennifer, author.
Title: Muffled / Jennifer Gennari.
Description: First edition. | New York : Simon & Schuster Books for Young Readers,
[2020] | Audience: Ages 8-12. | Audience: Grades 4-6. | Summary: When fifth-grader
Amelia learns to cope with her noise sensitivity, she steps outside of her comfort zone
and makes new friends. Includes information about noise sensitivity.
Identifiers: LCCN 2020002272 | ISBN 9781534463653 (hardcover) |
ISBN 9781534463660 (pbk) | ISBN 9781534463677 (eBook)
Subjects: CYAC: Friendship—Fiction. | Hearing disorders—Fiction. | Schools—Fiction.
| Family life—Massachusetts—Boston—Fiction. | Boston (Mass.)—Fiction.
Classification: LCC PZ7.G29174 Muf 2020 | DDC [Fic]—dc23
LC record available at https://lccn.loc.gov/2020002272

For John Schlag, who taught me to listen.

MUFFLED

CHAPTER 1

On the other side of the lobby door, ninety-six sidewalk lines away, is the first day of fifth grade. I stare through the glass, tugging at my backpack straps, although they are fine. I know I am stalling. As soon as I open the door, the outside will rush into my ears: taxi horns, loud radios, barking dogs. I hold on to the quiet for as long as I can.

"Do you want us to walk with you?" Dad asks, right as Mom says, "Ready, Amelia?"

I shake my head. I savor one more moment of quiet—only to be interrupted by the elevator dinging. Deb brushes by us.

"See you there!" she says as she pushes open the

lobby door. Warm air and city commotion burst into our apartment building. I cover my ears and count the ways I am different this year:

1. I am ten now and can walk to school by myself.
2. Mom and Dad gave me a new CharlieCard and permission to ride the T alone to the Boston Public Library.
3. My noise-canceling headphones are not on my head.

Once the door closes, I lower my hands. Outside, I see Deb catch up to Jax, who lives across the street. They head off together, without me. I tell myself that's fine. I am only a neighborhood pal to Jax and, ever since third grade, backup friend to Deb-minus-Kiki.

I take a step toward the door, and then hesitate. I feel light-headed, missing the weight of my headphones. Only my hair covers my ears.

Mom hugs me good-bye. "Fifth grade will be great."

Dad touches my arm. "One more thing," he says, and hands me a box.

"What's this?" Mom asks, as surprised as I am.

I open it. Inside are purple earmuffs with a white band. I slip them on. The muffs—soft and furry—cover my ears completely. I love them instantly. Earmuffs are like having permission to place your hands over your ears all the time.

I hug Dad hard. He laughs.

Mom's smile doesn't quite reach her eyes. "Where did you get those?" she asks Dad.

"Target," he says.

I think she is really asking *why*, but I don't care. Now I am ready. I open the lobby door and walk by myself to school. Every few feet, I can't help touching the fluff over my ears. How wonderfully soft! My steps grow bold. I'm sure everyone is admiring my beautiful, regular-looking earmuffs.

At the end of the first block, the traffic light turns green and all the cars accelerate at once. I jump—it's louder than I expect. I walk eight more sidewalk lines, noticing city sounds more than before: the beeping of a backing-up truck, the one-sided cell phone conversations, the rattling of tires over potholes. The volume I hear is about five bars out of ten. Noise-canceling headphones are more like one bar. Earmuffs are better than nothing, though.

Under my earmuffs, at least, everything is muffled, every sound is bearable. Almost.

I stand in the doorway of room twelve. Mr. Fabian has gray hair pulled back in a ponytail, and he is in the front of the room checking off names. Jax spins a pencil in the air. Deb-and-Kiki talk loudly, in side-by-side desks. Madge stretches her long legs beyond her chair. Soon Noah, José, Emma, Lina—everyone— will fill the classroom with too many sounds. *Three rows with seven desks each is twenty-one.*

No one else looks changed. I am the one who is different, now that my headphones are gone and I'm wearing beautiful earmuffs. I take a deep breath, adjust the band, and step into the classroom.

Instead of ignoring me like usual, they stare at my head.

"New earmuffs?" Deb asks.

"Your head is smaller now!" Noah says.

"Yeah, you no longer look like you work at an airport!" Kiki says, which launches a laughter wave.

My face turns as hot as my ears under my muffs. I keep my eyes down until I find my name on a desk next to Madge. *My earmuffs are beautiful,* I remind myself as I sit, letting the soft fluff brush my shoulder.

4

The bell rings, and I jump, unprepared. I press hard on my muffed ears, eyes shut, as everyone drops backpacks, scrambles to desks, scrapes chair legs across the floor. Mr. Fabian claps twice and snaps three times and claps again. Everyone's hands make noise except mine. I am as stiff as a new book. Earmuffs do not cancel noise. Not even close.

"Welcome to fifth grade!" Mr. Fabian says, and announces that we'll do ten minutes of silent reading every day, starting now.

Ten minutes is not very long, but I'm happy for the promise of quiet. I choose a book off the shelf about a raccoon named Bingo. I turn to the first page and stare at the words, but I can't focus.

All around me are little pestering sounds. Jax curls the pages of his book, over and over like an itch. Cassie snorts and giggles as she reads, and even though Noah is three rows back and my earmuffs are on, I hear him popping gum. Madge says she doesn't have a book, and Mr. Fabian sends her to the bookcase. Her shoelace charms *clink-clank-plink* with every step. She knocks books around on the shelf, picking one up, dropping it, flipping through another. Each noise bounces around the walls of my head like a rubber ball.

Mr. Fabian keeps saying "Shh" over and over.

I close my eyes, place my hands over the muffs again, and fly in my mind to the Boston Public Library, where librarians catalog all sounds. *Inside voices, outside voices*, they say. It's where I can wrap myself in books like a blanket—

I feel a tap on my shoulder and open my eyes. Mr. Fabian is standing right next to me. "Amelia, how can you read with your eyes closed?"

Everyone turns to stare at me. I mumble, "How can I read with so much noise?"

Mr. Fabian pauses and bends down to speak so only I can hear. "I understand you're trying something new this year." He points to my earmuffs. "Are these part of the plan? Maybe you should take them off."

I shake my head. "I like my new earmuffs." Even with them, I feel as exposed as a bird on a wire.

I turn back to the page and pretend to read, hoping he will go away. *Please don't make everyone look at me again.* I'm relieved when Jax asks him a question.

Things are no better when it's time for my favorite subject. Mr. Fabian hands out fifth-grade math workbooks, but everyone asks him so many questions, he can't get started talking about geometry and twelve-digit place values and long division.

I write my name inside the cover, concentrating on each stroke of each letter to block out Noah's yawn, Lina's complaints, and Madge's groans. I flip through the clean pages, greeting the numbers like old friends.

At lunchtime, I clutch my brown bag, waiting near the door until the first rush of cafeteria noise dims: banging trays, ripping plastic, overtalking at too-crowded tables.

Shoulders tight, I take note of who sits where. Like last year, Deb is sitting with Kiki, Lina, and Emma. I see only their backs; everyone is clustered around Kiki. Her voice is sharp like a crow's. In fourth grade, I tried to follow Deb into that circle, but it didn't widen to include me.

Jax sits with Noah and Madge. Madge talks with an open mouth, and I see her chewed-up sandwich. She laughs hard when Noah burps after he guzzles chocolate milk. Some spills onto his shirt.

Nothing has changed. Except me. I touch my earmuffs again, so light on my head.

I walk the cafeteria perimeter to my table from last year, in the corner near the trash and recycling bins. I open my lunch bag and my copy of *Alanna,* even though I've read it five times. This way, no one will talk to me, and I can eat fast.

When it's recess, I head to my place on the playground: inside the tube tunnel, my burrow. I curl up against the curve, back on hard plastic, knees near my eyes. Through the earmuffs I can still hear Kiki's exaggerated screams, the creak of the swings, and Madge's shouts of "You missed me. . . . No, not me! You're it!" in a game of tag. But at least purple fluff cushions the noise.

I hear footsteps climbing up into the tube. Jax appears, but he stops when he sees me like a clog in a pipe. We stare at each other for a moment before he backs down the ladder, leaving me alone, like last year. It's like my earmuffs are stop signs. Which is fine, I tell myself. Now I don't have to share my tunnel.

Mr. Fabian asks everyone to make fall leaves for the bulletin board and to write our names on them. We will post our creations by our leaves all year. On each desk are scissors and orange, yellow, red paper. "Quiet conversation is okay during art," he says.

No, I think, but it's too late. Talk surges around me like someone turned on twenty-one radios inside my head. I hear Cassie's voice overlapping with Tyler's on top of Ryan's. I press my muffs firmly on my ears.

Kiki taps me on the shoulder. I cautiously lower my hands, wondering why she's talking to me.

"Is it snowing?" Kiki asks. Deb dramatically arches her neck to peer over Kiki's shoulder.

I turn toward the windows. Outside, the street trees are starting to turn orange-yellow, matching our bright artwork.

"It's fall," I say to Deb-and-Kiki.

Kiki points at my head. "Then why are you wearing earmuffs inside?"

Everyone laughs.

"I can wear whatever I want," I say, but no one pays attention.

By the time the last bell rings, I make up my mind. I will wear my earmuffs at lunch, at recess, at the library, when I take math tests. I will say, *The headband holds my hair back*, and I will wear them every day until no one notices them anymore.

Fifth grade will be the year of earmuffs.

CHAPTER 2

After school, when Dad gets home, he says we have to go to the store. I'd rather stay on the sofa, but shopping is easier together. I drag our rolling cart into the elevator and jam my earmuffs back on.

Scuto's Market is five blocks away. We walk past the brick buildings and under the trees that shade our street. Even though I've just walked these same blocks, it's nicer with Dad. We match our strides, concentrating on our feet.

"So . . . how was school?" Dad asks.

"It's really different." I pause. "Lunch was the worst. All the conversations crashed together." I don't tell him about un-silent reading.

"Ah yes, like cars without a stoplight." Dad smashes his hands together. We walk two more sidewalk lines before he asks, "Do you like the earmuffs?"

"Yes." I remember Kiki's words stinging my ears. "They will be extra nice when it's colder," I add. When it's winter, my earmuffs won't stand out as much.

"I thought they would help." He stops at the door of Scuto's. "Ready?"

I nod, adjusting my earmuffs band. I know what's coming. Dad and I each take a deep breath before stepping through the door.

As soon as we're inside, all the sounds ambush me. The background music is one more irritation on top of squeaky shopping cart wheels, and people asking "Do you have shallots?" and "Where is the kosher salt?" Someone is on their phone asking how to cook lentils. The guy at the fish counter is tossing words back and forth with a woman, about what's fresh and what's a good deal today.

The aisles are narrow, and the shelves are full of so many cans, boxes, tins, and jars. It's impossible for two people to browse side by side. Dad and I move toward and away from the shelves, like hopping bugs, trying to make a buffer of space between us and other shoppers.

A baby starts crying, and I press against Dad. I don't know how he manages without anything over his ears. At least we are in this together.

He bends down, just like Mr. Fabian. "Play the counting game," he whispers. "Concentrate on only one thing at a time. It will help."

Dad is methodical, examining each item before he adds it to our cart. I do the same. I count what we have: one box of pasta, one container of orange juice, and one loaf of bread equals three. Add five zucchini and three onions to make eleven. My breathing slows, and finally we have everything on the list.

Checking out is a challenge too. The staff call out "Next in line!" and shake open paper bags that crackle. The scanner *beep, beep, beep*s for every purchase, and Dad exchanges mindless words with the clerk about the weather. I place the bags in our rolling cart to keep us moving. As soon as we are out on the sidewalk, we both lower our shoulders at the same time and notice and laugh.

There is no need for conversation on the walk home. Dad knows I am counting pavement lines, and he is looking through the leaves on the trees for birds.

"Pigeon," he says after a few blocks. "Chickadee." He points to a small bird on a branch.

"Seventeen sidewalk cracks," I say.

Dad smiles. "Isn't it nice the way numbers can keep you company?"

I smile too and continue counting until we are back at our brick apartment building. Twenty-two lines per block, *twenty times five blocks is one hundred, and two times five is ten.* One hundred and ten lines from Scuto's to home, same as always, a satisfying certainty.

The lobby door closes with a whoosh behind us. At last, it's safe to take my earmuffs off. We ride the elevator up.

Home is only-child quiet. Sounds come here one at a time. Dad listens to the Red Sox on low, making dinner. I chop zucchini. We take turns speaking. We move as quietly as Finway, our goldfish.

The apartment door opens, and Mom comes in. "Hello," she says low, slipping off her shoes. She kisses us both.

"How was the first day?" she asks me. "How is fifth grade?"

It takes me a moment to tune in to her question.

I'm distracted by how Mom's energy changes the air. It's not unwelcome. It's just different from when it's only me and Dad. She looks at me expectantly.

"My teacher, Mr. Fabian, is nice," I say. "We're going to learn how to multiply *multiple* digits."

That makes both my parents smile. Mom asks, "Who's in your class? Deb?"

"Deb-and-Kiki," I correct her. "My desk is next to Madge. She has charms on her shoelaces."

I place three forks and three plates on the table without clanking. I wonder if Madge walks around her home jangling.

Mom stops unpinning her name tag from her jacket. "You took the earmuffs off in class, right?"

I shake my head. "Even silent reading wasn't silent. And the cafeteria is really loud." I don't know how to explain that even with my earmuffs on, I heard sounds crashing and competing.

"Fifth grade will be a medley of new things." Dad is grinning as he mixes the zucchini, tomatoes, and yellow squash together.

"Ha ha," I say. "Except vegetables aren't noisy, Dad."

"Fifth grade will be a big year to grow up," Mom says.

I ignore her. I already proved I can be trusted to walk to school by myself.

We sit down to eat. The heat from the oven makes our kitchen cozy, and our table for three feels complete. I fork one zucchini, one yellow squash, and one tomato. I eat them in trios like that.

"Did anyone notice you weren't wearing headphones?" Mom asks.

"Of course. Earmuffs are smaller," I say. "And purple."

"It'll take time to get used to everything," Dad says.

"Well, try not to wear the earmuffs too much," Mom insists.

I stab the last zucchini. Mom makes it sound like I can wake up and decide to go to school without them, like not wearing socks one day. As if blistered heels—or blistered ears—are no big deal. Because that's what it would be like. Sound rubbing my brain raw.

After dinner, I press my nose against the glass fishbowl to greet Finway, eye to eye. Then I flop onto the sofa and pull out my homework. I've solved two problems when I hear Mom say my name in the kitchen. I listen, my pencil still.

"The world is noisy," Mom says. "She's going to have to get used to it. Those earmuffs were a mistake. We told the school she'd stop wearing headphones."

"She has," Dad says. "Her earmuffs will help her adjust."

"What about Mr. Skerritt's advice last year?"

"We're doing what the school counselor said, reducing reliance," Dad says. "She's still young, our Amelia Mouse. I am trying to help. What's wrong with that?"

I put my earmuffs back on with a snap, and their voices fall to a low undercurrent. Dad is wrong—I am not a mouse. And Mom is wrong. I will decide— on my own—what sounds I want to hear. And I will wear my earmuffs every day.

I watch Finway swim in his bowl. Dad says goldfish sense sound vibrations through their inner ear and the lines of sensory organs down their sides. He says he and I are like the fish. Too much sound, and our heads vibrate out of control. Mom is not a fish, not even close. She doesn't understand that my earmuffs are here to stay.

"Good night," I whisper to Finway, covering his bowl with his night cloth. I slip away to finish my homework in my room alone.

For the rest of the night the only sounds are the sounds I decide to make: writing numbers, spitting toothpaste, walking like a cat to my room, closing my bedroom door, flipping pages. No surprises.

I close my book and glance at my purple earmuffs on my dresser. My old black noise-canceling headphones are stashed in a box on the top shelf of my closet. Even covered with stickers, they look like they came from a hospital. When I wore them every day, they covered my ears completely. I listened to my thoughts. I heard the words I read or the numbers I counted in my head. When someone spoke to me, I'd have to take my headphones off. I'd say, *What?* Sometimes they jabbed my arm to get my attention. After a while, people stopped talking to me, even Deb.

When Deb and I were really little, we draped blankets over chairs while our moms sipped tea in the kitchen. Sometimes we pretended we had to be quiet to hide from dragons. But sometimes Deb stood on a chair and belted out a warrior cry. That was when my headphones would go back on. And I never took them off once school started. Then Kiki moved here, and Deb became Deb-and-Kiki.

I turn my light off, welcoming nighttime, when

most sounds sleep. I'm glad Dad gave me earmuffs. If only they could act more like a filter, blocking words I don't want to hear. And letting nice ones through.

One more thought slips in, unwanted, as I shut my eyes: *My only friend not in a book is a fish.*

CHAPTER 3

"Welcome to music!" Ms. Parker says when everyone from room twelve arrives. The music room is large, with double doors and no windows. "This year you'll learn to play an instrument!"

Worry gathers between my ears, which are warm under my muffs. Music by definition is making sound. I find a chair near the back wall.

Ms. Parker wears a long sweater as loose as her hair around her face. She opens a closet and takes out three different-shaped cases—little, medium, and long. She twists together metal pieces with holes for noise to come out, assembling three instruments. She explains that she teaches trombone, Ms.

Min flute, Mr. Tingle trumpet, and Mrs. Spitz directs the choir.

"Listen." Ms. Parker blows into the flute, and it makes a bubbly stream of high-pitched sound. I place my hands on my already covered ears, elbows straight out. She picks up the trumpet, and when she presses her lips to the brass, her three fingers make a loud parade of blaring notes. Last, she slides the long piece of the trombone all the way to her knees and back, making a thundering sound. When she's done, I count to five before I ease my hands down.

"Think carefully about what you'd like to play," she says. "If you choose one of the three instruments, I have rental forms here to take home to your parents. We'll begin next week."

Deb-and-Kiki say "Flute!" at the exact same moment, and then "Jinx!" and laugh.

"Trumpet for me," Noah, José, and Jayden shout all together.

Most of the girls pick flute, except Madge. "I want to learn trombone," she says, and stands up to slide her arms down low as if she is playing already. She doesn't seem to care if she's the only girl in trombone class.

My stomach clenches. I will not choose flute. I will not play trumpet or trombone.

I raise my hand. "What if you don't want to learn an instrument?"

"You can join choir," Ms. Parker says. "Your voice box is an instrument too."

Jax waves his hand high. "I want to be in choir!"

I close my mouth, sink back into my chair, sweaty and tense. I can't imagine me—even with earmuffs on—shoulder to shoulder with everyone, making noise on *purpose*.

After lunch, back in room twelve, everyone keeps talking about music. Jayden plays air guitar, and Madge dances, jingling her shoelace chimes.

"I already play piano," Cassie says. "That's why I chose choir."

"I'm going to sing like Stevie Wonder," Jax says.

"Why can't I learn drums?" Noah complains.

"Sit down, everyone," Mr. Fabian says, "and open your social studies books."

We take turns reading paragraphs out loud about the thirteen colonies, and then Mr. Fabian hands out worksheets. "Answer the questions as best you can," he says.

I can't concentrate, pausing after every sentence I write. No way am I playing an instrument. Ms. Parker said I could tell her on Monday, but no matter what I choose, music class will be a disaster. I put my pencil down and drop my head into my hands.

"What's up, Amelia?" Mr. Fabian squats down next to me.

I lower my earmuffs. "Do I have to learn an instrument?"

"Does that worry you?" he asks.

I nod, hoping he will make an exception. He must know that making music is out of the question for me.

He pats the page. "Finish this, and we'll come up with a plan after class."

Maybe I will be excused from music! The thought excites me, and I finish the worksheet fast. For fun, I take out the weekly spelling list and start writing the words backward, sounding them out in my head:

"Boycott" is *T-toc-yob.*

"Colonial" is *Lain-o-loc.*

"Representative" is *Evitat-nes-erper.*

"Revolution" is *Noi-tu-lover.*

It makes me giggle. I look around. Deb is still working on her sentences, like Kiki. Jax is pressing down hard as he writes. Noah has stuck his pencil through a block eraser and keeps tapping it on his desk. No one asks me what's funny.

"Partner up," Mr. Fabian says. "It's time to practice spelling."

Everyone pairs off: Deb-and-Kiki, Ryan and José, Emma and Lina, Cassie and Jayden, desk to desk. And even though I'm next to Madge, she scoots over to Jax. I push my earmuffs back on as her chair screeches across the floor away from me.

Mr. Fabian notices that I am the odd one out. "Amelia," he says, "work with Tyler and Noah."

Noah frowns. "Why us?"

"The three of you will be a group," Mr. Fabian says, as if that is an answer.

I move over. Noah begins: "*B-o-y-c-o-t*. Get it? Boys only," which makes Tyler laugh.

I don't point out that he's spelled it wrong. Instead I keep my earmuffs on, keep my eyes on the words, eager for the end of the day.

Mr. Fabian's plan is not what I had hoped.

Instead of asking Ms. Parker to excuse me from music, he called a meeting after school with Mr. Skerritt. Mom had to leave her job at the hotel early to come.

We all cram into the counseling office, and Mom sits in the small chair next to me. Mr. Fabian stands. The office is barely large enough for four people, especially when three of them are adults.

It feels like I'm back in fourth grade, when I saw Mr. Skerritt every month. Mom gives me a look, and I take off my earmuffs and nervously hold them.

"Thanks for coming, everyone," Mr. Skerritt says. He wheezes when he speaks, like I remember. Last year, I used to stare at the posters on the wall and try to block out the sound of his breathing while he waited for me to talk about my feelings. The posters haven't changed. There's YOU MATTER and the one that says MISTAKES ARE PROOF YOU ARE TRYING.

"Let's review my notes from last June." Mr. Skerritt peers through old glasses at some pages. They are in a fat folder with my name at the top. "Ah yes. Like a security blanket, Amelia was using her noise-canceling headphones to soothe her sound sensitivity, making her social isolation worse."

Mr. Skerritt's ears are big. A few hairs poke out of one. "Social isolation," Mom had explained to me last year, means "difficulty making friends." I should remind everyone I *do* have friends—they just live in stories, that's all.

Now Mr. Skerritt addresses Mom and Mr. Fabian. "We recommended that fifth grade would be a good year for Amelia to reduce her reliance on the headphones."

He's talking about me as if I am not here. Like I am part of the chair. I stare at the poster over Mom's head and count how many words are on it (six).

"Yes," Mom says. "That's why this year, we've put them away."

"And the earmuffs?" Mr. Skerritt's disapproving gaze shifts to me. My fingers dig into the purple fluff.

"They're temporary," Mom says. "My husband thought they would help her adjust."

Mr. Fabian turns to me. "Amelia, are the earmuffs helping?"

"I like them." If Dad were here, he'd explain. But this meeting is not supposed to be about earmuffs or headphones. I ask what I really want to know. "Do I have to take music class?"

"It may be hard, but I think it will be good for you," Mr. Fabian says.

"Ah, yes, to acclimate to everyday sounds," Mr. Skerritt murmurs. He makes a note and then opens his calendar. "If you don't go to music, we could use that time slot to meet." He leaks a long rattling breath through his nose, which makes me shrink into my chair.

I grip my earmuffs, wishing I could snap them on right now. I look at Mom for help. The last thing I want is to get pulled from class again to talk about feelings. Fortunately, for once, Mom figures out what I'm thinking.

"Amelia, what do you say you promise to give music a chance?" Mom says. "And a little less earmuff-wearing during school, okay?"

I will try anything to get out of meetings with Mr. Skerritt and his noisy breathing. Even singing. "I promise," I say. "I'll join choir."

"Great," Mr. Fabian says. "I'm glad we're all in agreement. Amelia and I will check back with you, Mr. Skerritt, and we'll see how it goes."

I'm so happy to be out of the small room and excused from Mr. Skerritt. But I didn't really win. I still have to sing.

CHAPTER 4

As we enter the choir room, Mrs. Spitz plays heavy chords on the piano. "Pair off, everyone," she says, "and get ready to sing!"

I hold my earmuffs to my ears and move toward the back. All weekend I thought of my promise to Mom and Mr. Fabian and Mr. Skerritt. I know I have to sing, but I didn't expect it to be in the first five minutes. I breathe in through my nose.

Who will be my partner? I look around. Jax is already standing next to Ryan. Cassie has linked arms with someone from the other fifth-grade classroom. More people signed up for choir than I expected. *Five people in front, plus four on my right side, including me, plus six on my left equals fifteen.*

Two goes into fifteen seven times with one leftover—me.

Mrs. Spitz doesn't seem to notice. She is short, and her white hair flies like her hands on the piano keys as she tells us about the four parts of a choir. "Sopranos sing the highest notes, altos lower." She strikes tinkling notes at the top of the keyboard and then ones in the middle. "Tenors are higher than basses," she says, "which is easy to remember because basses are in the basement."

Everyone laughs at the deep thunder she plays on the piano. I don't. I crush my earmuffs to my head.

Mrs. Spitz stands up. "Our choir will only have two parts, soprano and alto." She sings "La, la, la," her voice rising up steps like a ladder. "Everyone, sing with me!"

The la, la, las are about a seven out of ten, so I keep my hands on my earmuffs. I can't open my mouth.

"Now let's see where your voices naturally fall." She begins to work around the room, moving from pair to pair, listening to the singing. She sorts each of us, sopranos to the right, altos to the left. I keep inching left, to avoid Mrs. Spitz's pointing fingers.

"La, la, la," Mrs. Spitz sings again, and the same rising notes are echoed back. I am amazed to hear that Jax's voice is clear and sweet. His wide-open mouth looks like Finway's. Mine is the opposite: balled up like a sock in the laundry.

Mrs. Spitz stops when she reaches me. "Amelia, is it?" she asks.

I nod. Everyone stares at me. I wish I could burrow into the wall.

"So wonderful to have you in choir," she says. "Can you be brave and take off your earmuffs and sing a little bit?"

I look at my feet. *It isn't being brave,* I want to say. It's foolish to slide down my muffs, with all the noise in the room. I slowly lower them anyway.

"I'll do it with you so you don't have to sing alone," she says. "And, sing! La, la, la."

I part my lips, but no sound comes out. A few snickers fill the silence. I close my mouth. What I need are invisibility earmuffs.

"That's all right. I'll place you later." Mrs. Spitz pats me on the shoulder as if I'm a pet. I flinch.

"Beautiful, beautiful!" Her words bounce up and down as she sits at the piano again. "Now we have a choir!"

I don't know where to stand. Jax is in the middle, so I slide behind him.

"Let's start with something you all know," Mrs. Spitz says. She plays the first notes of the national anthem, and everyone sings as if we are at Fenway, shouting to fill the stadium. The "rockets' red glare" high part explodes in my ears, and my shoulders tense at "bombs bursting in air." I jam my earmuffs back on. "Land of the free" lands like a screech.

My mouth is dry, hands hard against my muffed ears. There is no space around me, no space left in my head. Everyone presses in and I'm trapped, like I'm in a crowded elevator.

I will not sing. I will not add to the noise.

As the last note dies, Mrs. Spitz walks over to me, and all eyes turn my way. My stomach squeezes. Why can't she pretend I'm not here?

"Are you okay? I didn't see you singing." Her voice is sweetened like when grown-ups talk to babies. "I'd like to see you try, Amelia. And with no earmuffs."

Everyone's gaze is like a hundred headlights. I cross my legs even though it is my throat that is constricted. "May I be excused?" I ask, my voice wobbly.

"Sure." She pats me on the shoulder again and returns to the piano bench. "From the top," she says, and the class starts singing again.

The sounds spray against my head as I rush out. I close the door on the bellowing choir. The sudden silence in the hallway rings in my ears. I take one, two, three deep breaths. My sneakers squeak against polished floor, and I move slowly until my ears calm down.

One thing is certain. I can't be in choir without earmuffs.

Lunch is nearly over. I've barricaded myself behind my book and under my earmuffs. It works—no one notices me. If only I could stop picturing Mrs. Spitz patting me. And stop hearing the national anthem in my head.

I get up to sort my lunch trash into the recycling, compost, and waste cans. I've waited too long, though. The corner is crowded, and people bump into each other, rushing to clean up before we go to recess.

A shove—someone rams the trash can. It clatters over, spewing garbage. Everyone screams, "Eww!"

The sudden shout pushes me over the edge. I drop my book, press my hands hard against my earmuffed ears. I back away, run outside, straight to my tube.

Count, Dad always says. *Breathe.*

Three grades times two classes times twenty kids is one hundred and twenty. One hundred and twenty kids with two pieces of trash each is two hundred forty things to throw away.

My breathing slows. *Two hundred and forty divided by three trash cans is eighty. Eighty items pouring from one knocked-over bin is gross.*

A gentle knock on plastic. Madge is standing on the ladder at the mouth of my tunnel.

"Here," she says, and hands me back my book.

I blink my eyes, my throat tight. She turns and climbs down before I can manage to say thanks.

It's unexpected to be seen.

The final bell rings on cue. I've memorized the bell schedule so that I can always be prepared to hold my hands over my muffed ears.

On the school steps, Madge sings out, "Can't wait to get home! Oma's always cooking something."

"Cake? Cookies?" Jax asks. As if he's angling to come over. I'm hungry too.

"Not sweets. My grandmother usually makes sausage. Bratwurst is not the worst!" Madge laughs. Jax joins in.

Their laughter is nice and warm, like a bowl of soup. I am not quite next to Jax and Madge, and yet maybe I can say thank you now to her for returning my book. But first I turn over in my mind which snack I should mention—peanut butter banana or tomato soup.

I take too long. Madge is down the stairs and turning onto her street. Jax runs to catch up with Deb. The moment to say anything is gone. If you listen but don't speak, are you even in the conversation?

Slowly I head for home, counting the lines and cataloging all the loud sounds my earmuffs don't really muffle: cab honks, bus brakes, slammed doors.

Today my earmuffs are blinders too: I pretend I don't see Jax and Deb walking together a block ahead without me.

After dinner, Mom suggests stoop sitting. I do not want to go outside, but Dad says I can wear my earmuffs, so I agree. The three of us sit on the top step to our apartment building, Dad in the middle. It's warm with a crisp wind, a signal that nights will soon be colder and darker.

"Isn't this perfect?" Mom sighs and leans into Dad's shoulder. "Fall is here."

"It is," he says, then tugs on my earmuff band. "Listen."

I take down my earmuffs slowly. I hear cars, of course, and someone's radio playing. A dog barks somewhere, and a bicyclist goes by, small tires crunching on pavement. The wind moves the changing leaves in the trees.

"Doo, doo." Dad sings two notes over and over. "Doo, doo."

I find the small bird in the tree overhead. "Chickadee."

"A beautiful song," Mom murmurs.

The chickadee sings again. A truck growls by, a trash can lid bangs shut, reminding me of the sound of the trash bin toppling at lunch. I slide my earmuffs back up. One bird singing is bearable but not with the other sounds happening all at once. I don't know how Dad has trained himself to concentrate only on one bird call amid all the outside noise.

"Amelia, how was choir?" Mom asks.

I can't tell her I hated it, or that Mrs. Spitz is anti-earmuffs, or that she patted me on the shoulder twice. I'm afraid if Mom knows, she will send me to Mr. Skerritt again.

"Fine," I say, muffling my lie into Dad's other shoulder.

"What did you sing?" Mom asks.

"The national anthem," I say. "It was like at Fenway."

Dad looks at me sideways. "Was that a good or bad thing—"

"That's fun!" Mom interrupts, and starts singing.

"Stop!" I say.

A hurt expression crosses Mom's face.

"Amelia, there's no need to yell," Dad says. "What happened?"

"When we're at Fenway, the song floats away into the sky," I explain. "Inside, the song had nowhere to go."

"That sounds loud," Dad says. "Did the earmuffs help?"

"Sort of," I lie again.

"But singing is a good sound, isn't it?" Mom insists.

"When everyone is in tune," Dad says with a grin.

A truck rumbles down the street, and I scrunch my shoulders up. When it's quiet enough to talk again, Mom thankfully starts telling a story about dealing with a room mix-up at the hotel.

Voices out of tune are not the problem. I look across the street to where Jax lives and remember how nice his voice sounded. If I only had to listen to him instead of fifteen voices, maybe choir would be okay. But choir isn't about listening. Mrs. Spitz will expect me to sing. I promised to try. But I can't.

Learning music will be the fourth way—after turning ten, after getting a CharlieCard, after no more headphones—that I am different this year. And maybe that's one thing too many for fifth grade.

Finally the evening chill sends us inside. Brushing my teeth, I decide what to do. I won't say anything to Mom and Dad. I don't want an argument. I will fix my choir problem by myself.

CHAPTER 5

From the first bell the next day, I start counting how long until choir. *Ten minutes of silent reading plus fifty of math plus fifty of social studies before music class, equals one hundred and ten minutes.* I keep hearing in my head Mrs. Spitz's opening chords like the march of doom. I can't go again.

At ten fifteen, the bell rings. Everyone gets up. I am stuck in my chair.

"I can't go to choir anymore," I say when Mr. Fabian realizes I am still in room twelve.

"Is there something wrong?" he asks.

"I couldn't sing yesterday," I whisper. "Everyone else was already singing so loudly."

He erases the board slowly, then says, "I could use a helper next period, just this one time."

I exhale. I hadn't realized I was holding my breath. "Can I boycott music class for the rest of the year?" I add, hoping to win a smile for using a spelling word.

He puts the eraser down. "And see Mr. Skerritt instead?"

The thought makes me go still. "I'll try an instrument. Anything but choir."

"Why was it so terrible?"

I touch the purple fluff on my head. "Mrs. Spitz won't let me wear earmuffs."

"You'll have to tell Ms. Parker," Mr. Fabian says. "And, Amelia, Mrs. Spitz was probably trying to help you not wear earmuffs too much."

I nod, but he doesn't understand. Mrs. Spitz doesn't either. I have to wear the earmuffs every day. Stubbornly, I keep them on, even though it's perfectly quiet in the classroom now. The only sound is the rhythmic *thunk, thunk, thunk* as I staple math worksheets, three pages for twenty-one students. Sixty-three pages. Sometimes I stop to pull out a bent one and neatly stack the pages again to staple them just right.

• • •

At lunch, I wait at the cafeteria entrance until the first rush of sound drops. That's when I notice people coming straight from flute or trumpet class and sitting together at new tables. More girls are sitting with Deb-and-Kiki.

I walk over and sit in my usual spot, unwrap my sandwich, and focus on Alanna's story. But even though I am sitting at my same table with my same lunch and the same book the way I like, something feels not right.

I touch my head. My earmuffs are on snugly. No one looks over at me or interrupts my reading. For once, I wish they would, so I could tell them about the decision I have to make. I won't be in choir with Jax anymore. What should I choose? Flutes are small but squeaky. Trumpets are medium-size but loud. Trombones are mellower but large. Will everyone playing together sound like a twenty-car traffic jam?

Outside, across the playground, I see the one tall pine tree, branches lifted above the school's brick wall. Its green needles stand out among the yellow-and-orange maple trees. That's me. That's where I'd like to be, floating high above the noise.

• • •

Still undecided, I go to talk to Ms. Parker at the end of the day. The music room is not empty. A few people are picking up instruments to take home. Deb-and-Kiki are showing Ms. Parker a new piece they learned, blowing rippling notes like jungle birds.

I wait, muffs over ears.

Madge, who won't be upstaged, unpacks her trombone and blows one *blat* like a big fart, and my hands fly to my ears. Noah laughs so hard that spit flies off his lips.

"Gross!" Deb says, and I realize I'd rather play a sweet instrument than a gross one.

At last, when the room is empty, I stand in front of Ms. Parker's desk. "I don't want to be in choir," I say. I wish I could tell her I want no music class at all. But I promised Mr. Skerritt. And Mom. And Mr. Fabian.

She sighs but doesn't look surprised. "You still have to learn to read music," she says. "Which instrument do you want to try?"

I remember the trills Deb made, fingers light on her flute. They sounded like birds, and I think of Dad, counting the birds in the trees.

While I'm thinking, Ms. Parker adds, "I have some older ones you can borrow for free if you want to try them out before renting."

"Thanks." I hadn't thought about the cost.

Maybe the flute teacher is different from Mrs. Spitz. I ask, "Will Ms. Min let me wear my earmuffs sometimes?"

"I could ask." Ms. Parker pauses. "But only when it gets to be too much."

"Flute," I say. "I'll try flute."

The next day in room twelve, Mr. Fabian has on a Red Sox cap. "Today we will figure out Mookie Betts's batting average," he says.

Jax's hand is up. "It's two ninety-nine!" If math were about the Red Sox, Jax would know all the answers.

"True!" Mr. Fabian says. "Today, though, we're going to pretend these are his statistics." He writes on the board *career hits = 150* and *at-bats = 500*.

He turns back to the class. "Batting averages are determined by number of hits divided by at-bats."

I wrinkle my nose, thinking. I take off the zeros and see fifteen over fifty. To make the fraction smaller, I know that both numbers are multiples of five. Seven and twenty-one, and seven goes into twenty-one three times.

"That's too hard," Madge protests.

"Can we use a calculator?" Jax asks.

"Anyone?" Mr. Fabian waits.

I slide down my earmuffs and raise my hand. "There are three fives in fifteen, and five fives in fifty. The answer is three over ten, which is three hundred, right?"

Mr. Fabian writes 3/10 equals point three hundred on the board.

Madge is amazed. "Whoa! How did you know so fast?"

"I'm not surprised," Deb announces. "Amelia's always talking numbers."

I'm happy Deb says that; it's a little sign that she still knows me. I doodle my name backward: *Ailema, Ailema, Ailema*, sounding it out in my head, becoming someone else, a flute player, someone who fits in.

The flute is silver, heavy in my hands. I stretch to put fingers on the right keys. The metal is cold.

Ms. Min stands in front of the eleven of us—I counted—all girls, standing and ready to play. Ms. Min wears black and a serious expression, as if she has just come from a concert performance.

"Put your lower lip under the hole and roll it

up and blow," she says. Then she quickly adds "Just Amelia," but it's too late—the room swells with shrieks, toots, wails, and whistles.

I press one earmuffed ear against my shoulder and manage not to flee or drop the flute. Ms. Min holds up her hand. Everyone stops.

"Watch how I hold my flute, Amelia," she says. "Don't kiss it!"

Deb-and-Kiki giggle. I concentrate on the placement of my fingers. Ms. Min tells me which finger goes on which key.

"Good. Now leave your lips open and blow a steady stream of air across the hole like this." Ms. Min does it, and the sound is sweet and full.

Ms. Min and I blow together, one finger up. All I hear from mine is air. I adjust my lips and try again. This time, I don't sound too bad. Deb smiles encouragement when Kiki isn't looking. Next to me, Lina plays a perfect note, mimicking Ms. Min. I try again, and it sounds a little less breathy.

Maybe I can make this flute sing like a happy bird, after all.

At the end of the day I wait by the school steps, hand tight on the handle of my small flute case. I watch everyone leaving, some walking, some waiting for rides. Kiki says good-bye to Deb, and then I follow as Deb and Jax head down our street.

I swing my black case, two steps behind them the whole way. Jax is talking about how the popcorn at Fenway is better than homemade. I'm listening, but I also hear rushing cars, wind blowing leaves from trees. All ninety-six lines home, I practice a question for Deb in my head.

"Want to play catch?" I hear Jax say as we get close to our apartment buildings.

Deb tosses him a dismissive look. "I've outgrown that, Jax."

"Whatever," he says, shrugging. You can tell that Deb's answer doesn't bother him. Jax crosses the street to his building. I like throwing a baseball back and forth, but not today. I'm glad Deb said no, because now I can ask her my question.

When Deb and I are safe inside the lobby, I lower my earmuffs and take a deep breath. "Want to practice flute together?"

She pauses for one beat, two beats. "Sure, why not?"

"Great," I say. "Let's go to my apartment."

My plan worked! It feels like we are in third

grade again, pre-Kiki. We get off on my floor, and I unlock the door to home. This is the beginning of the new me.

I drop my backpack and earmuffs onto the sofa. "Hello, Finway," I say, and shake a few food flakes on top. Deb gets close to the bowl and says hi too. She remembers not to startle him.

In my room, we screw together flute pieces: mouthpiece into body into tail.

"Lina is the best player. Have you noticed?" Deb says. "Kiki and I are trying to be as good as she is."

"I hope I can catch up fast," I say. I put my fingers in the right places and blow across the hole. The sound comes out soft and breathy.

"That's not right," Deb says. "Blow harder, like this." She sends strong air across the silver hole, rippling her fingers up and down the keys like lightning.

Her too-close trill jolts me like thunder. I throw my flute onto the bed, crush my hands against my ears.

Deb stops. I'm hunched over as I try to recover. She studies me. "What happened to those big airport headphones you used to wear?"

The ringing in my ears wanes. I remove my

hands, drop my shoulders. I'm sorry I left my ear-muffs by my backpack.

"I don't need them anymore," I say, and pick up the flute again. I blow one low note to convince myself.

"If you say so." She runs through "Twinkle, Twinkle, Little Star." I try to keep from wincing. I start at the beginning, and we play the song together. I count three mistakes I make. Deb makes zero mistakes.

"I'm hungry. Are you?" she asks, as if she's done.

I'm fine with only five minutes of practice, especially when I'm so bad in comparison. In the kitchen, we slice peeled bananas the long way and smear peanut butter onto the flat sides like glue.

"I'll get better," I say. "At flute playing, I mean."

"Kiki and I usually practice with each other," Deb says. "She's shopping with her mom today."

I press my banana halves together. "Maybe I can practice with both of you," I suggest quietly.

Deb licks peanut butter off her finger before answering. "Her house is far, and Kiki has a dog who barks a lot. You wouldn't like it."

Deb isn't looking at me when she says this. I push on my banana slices again, too hard this time, and peanut butter squirts out. No words come to mind, so I take a bite and make banana-filled chipmunk cheeks.

"Don't be so babyish," Deb says, disgusted. She takes a small bite of her peanut butter banana.

I swallow. My throat closes up and I blink hard. I can't cry. Then I'll really be a baby.

Deb keeps talking about Kiki's big house and how they always have cookies and pretzels and ice cream to eat. I keep trying to come up with something to say, but nothing seems right, and I reject so many words I end up staying silent. Once we've eaten our bananas, Deb goes home.

When the door closes behind her, I'm not sorry to be alone again, me and Finway, who never makes trouble.

CHAPTER 6

The door opens, Dad blows me a kiss, and then he heads straight to the kitchen. "We're bringing Mom her dinner tonight."

I get up off the sofa slowly. So much for a quiet night at home. "She has to stay?"

He nods. "Help me make egg sandwiches."

I fill a pot of water and add in five eggs. When the water boils, I set the timer for twelve minutes. I line up six slices of bread and toast them, two at a time in the toaster.

"Why does Mom have to work late?" I butter the bread when the slices pop up.

"She took an extra shift," Dad says. He dices celery and scallions. "Anything new at school today?"

"Nope." With a start, I remember the flute case on my bed, right out in the open. If Dad sees it, he's going to wonder why. I'm not ready to talk about my solution to the choir problem. What if they are disappointed? I need to hide the flute.

"Are we taking the T?" I ask.

He nods. "Do you have your CharlieCard?"

"In my backpack." I zip to my room and slide the flute case under my bed. I'm not sure how I am going to tell them about choir. I find my Charlie-Card and put it in my pocket.

When the eggs are done, Dad and I mash everything together with mayonnaise and mustard. We wrap the sandwiches in tinfoil, I snap on my earmuffs, and we head for the elevator.

It's dark and cold out. My earmuffs are perfect for the weather. We walk quickly, the warm sandwiches in a bag. At the turnstile, I insert my CharlieCard, push through, and take it out on the other side. It feels great to have my own, but I am worried. This is my first time on the T without noise-canceling headphones.

As the train pulls into the station, the squeal of the brakes makes me bury my head into Dad's side. We find seats on the downtown-bound train. The doors close, and the subway rocks and screeches along the tracks. The announcements are so loud that Dad and I both put our hands to our ears, me crushing fluff against my head. At Longwood Station, we take the steps fast out into the night air.

When we enter the fancy hotel where Mom works, I relax in the hushed lobby with the twinkling chandelier. Cautiously I lower my earmuffs. Mom is behind the registration desk. She looks official, with her name pinned to her dark jacket. She finishes helping a customer, then waves us into the staff room.

"My two favorite people!" she greets us. "Thank you for bringing me food and smiles." She kisses Dad.

"Amelia and I had a fine time riding the T," he says. "She broke in her new CharlieCard."

"The subway was loud," I add.

"Not too bad, I hope," Mom says. She brings us fizzy drinks from the staff refrigerator as a treat and slips out of her shoes. She sighs.

We unwrap our sandwiches and eat. It's like a picnic, sort of, except we are sitting at a round table under bright lights that buzz.

"Do you know why it's called a CharlieCard?" Mom asks me after a moment.

I shake my head.

Mom begins to sing: "Did he ever return? No, he never returned, and his fate is still unlearned. He may ride forever 'neath the streets of Boston."

"Mom!" I say, and cover my ears. It's embarrassing, and I wonder if anyone in the hotel hears her.

Dad laughs. "It's an old folk song. Charlie didn't have enough money to get off the T."

Mom snaps her fingers. "And his wife brings him a sandwich! Just like you brought to me!"

"That's cool." I like knowing the story behind my CharlieCard.

"Maybe Mrs. Spitz knows the song about Charlie and the MBTA," Mom continues. "Why don't you ask her?"

I take a big drink of soda, stalling. Mom lets the moment grow, waiting patiently for me to answer the question at my own pace. But that's not why I'm hesitating this time—I'm trying to think what to say. Finally I decide to tell the truth.

"I quit choir," I mumble.

"What? Why?" Dad asks.

Mom stiffens. "We told Mr. Fabian and Mr. Skerritt you would go to music class."

I straighten up in my seat. "Mrs. Spitz didn't understand me, that's why!" Now I don't care if anyone hears. "She didn't let me wear earmuffs."

"But you can't wear your earmuffs all the time—"

Dad holds up his hands, like a referee. He asks, "Amelia, you have to take music, right?"

"I already told Ms. Parker about choir," I say. "I picked flute instead."

Mom and Dad exchange glances. Dad asks, "Do we have to rent an instrument?"

I shake my head. "Ms. Parker has a donated one I'm using."

Dad exhales, and Mom announces, "Then, that's wonderful. Now you'll be in flute class with Deb."

"You mean Deb-and-Kiki," I say.

"You still know Deb, though," Mom says. "You've been friends forever!"

I shove my earmuffs back on and don't say: *Deb practices with Kiki. At her big house. With a dog.*

"Look at the time." Dad stands up. "Amelia, let's go home so Mom can work."

Dad and I walk silently back to the station. We let the *clackety-clack* of the T drown out any chance for conversation. The train whistle reminds me of the tooting sounds I made today. I can't give up on flute. Maybe I don't have to give up on Deb, either.

• • •

In flute class on Friday, I watch Deb and try to follow her fingers and look at the notes at the same time. The flaps on the flute hinge up and down like manhole covers blowing off steam. And I'm surrounded by squeaks so high, they pierce through my earmuffs.

We're learning a new piece, "Ode to Joy." Ms. Min stands next to me and points to where I should be on the page, her foot tapping, making me flustered. I can't remember which fingers cover which holes. I can't keep up.

For once, it's a relief when the bell rings. Dizzy from blowing, I pack my flute away. The only thing I do right is to nestle the three silver pieces into the correct spaces in the velvet case.

At lunch, Deb-and-Kiki head to the table where they always sit. I hesitate, my lunch bag in my hand. One part of me wants my quiet table time. But now I am a flute player, and maybe Mom is right. I lower my earmuffs and slide in next to Deb. She makes room.

"What are you eating?" Deb pulls out a tin, unsnaps the lid. Inside are tidy piles of hummus, carrot sticks, and edamame beans.

"Grilled cheese," I say. I unwrap the once-warm sandwich. "I made it myself."

"Cold?" Kiki asks, laughing. Emma and Lina

giggle. Deb joins in, then covers her mouth.

I'm stuck like cheese to bread with Deb-and-Kiki who are not-that-nice. I miss Deb-minus-Kiki. Except then I remember that all Deb talked about when we were practicing was Kiki.

I am at the wrong table. I glance over at my corner. It's empty. Two tables away, Jax and Noah and Madge are giggling and whispering, their heads almost touching.

I take another bite of my sandwich.

"I love playing our new song," Deb says. "All those sixteenth notes!"

"It's better when no one makes mistakes," Kiki adds.

I know she is looking at me. I keep my eyes down, chewing, pretending not to hear—

HONK blasts into my un-muffed ears.

We all scream. I jerk my hands to my head, knocking juice all over the table and onto Kiki's lap. She leaps up, shouting, "Look what you did!"

"Why do you always have to be so jumpy, Amelia!" Deb cries.

I turn away and see Noah holding his trumpet, Jax laughing. Madge is watching us, with a strange, solemn expression.

Kiki whirls and yells at Noah and Jax what I now know is the worst insult: "You are all such babies!"

My earmuffs are on fast, as fast as my feet taking me away from the Deb-and-Kiki table, away from everyone. I head outside, straight for my tube tunnel. *Two steps times six is twelve. Twelve times two is twenty-four steps to safety.*

I curl against the hard plastic. What if there is no right place for me in the cafeteria?

Footsteps on the ladder startle me. It's Madge.

"Noah didn't mean to make you spill. It was supposed to be a joke." She crawls in, forcing me to move over so she can join me.

Get out of my tunnel, I want to scream.

"You can sit with us sometime," Madge says. "Noah shares his snacks."

She keeps talking, even though I give her the silent treatment.

"That's his way of saying sorry, too." She pulls a candy bar from her pocket and holds it out. "He asked me to give you this."

I stare at the candy, not sure if I want to accept the peace offering.

"Go on, take it," Madge says. "At least he tries to apologize, unlike *some* people we know."

Is she thinking of Kiki, who never says sorry? I start to ask her what she means, but she scoots over more, and suddenly her hand is too close to my face and I shift away.

Madge lets out a long frustrated sigh. She stuffs the candy bar back into her pocket. "I don't know why you can't let people be nice to you, Amelia." She backs up, pushes herself out of the tunnel. She says, so loud that it echoes down the sides, "I guess you don't even want friends!"

And then she's gone, which is what I wanted, but somehow I am as hollow as my tube.

CHAPTER 7

It's Saturday morning, and already Dad has asked twice if I'm going to practice my flute today, and Mom has asked me three times if I want to get together with anyone.

I do not want to play flute. I do not want to run into Deb in the elevator. I do not want to be home with my parents and their pestering questions.

I know what I need—a new friend, waiting for me on a bookshelf at the Boston Public Library. After I do my homework, Mom says it's fine for me to go, although she complains a little about not getting to spend the day with me.

She walks me to the T station. "How is flute going?"

I shrug. I'm not ready to talk about anything.

Mom offers a few more conversation starters, but when I don't answer, she gives up. We walk the rest of the way without talking.

Outside the station, she asks, "Are you sure you don't want company?"

"I'm ten," I remind her. I am ready to go alone for the first time.

I swipe my CharlieCard and go through the turnstile. The next inbound green line train comes, and I step on board. I take a window seat, press against the glass.

Earmuffs barely reduce the *clackety-clack* noise. Teenagers talk in show-offy voices. An old man is blowing his nose. I keep my eyes on the stop map: Brookline, Longwood, Fenway. *Six, five, four*, I count down.

I tighten the headband on my earmuffs. I wish I had told Madge I do have friends. Hermione is one, and Alanna of Trebond. There is Miranda and Abilene and Esperanza and India Opal. *If you don't know them, your loss*, I should have said to Madge.

Friends in books are the best. They sleep in the pages when I don't want to talk, and they share their days with me soundlessly when I lift their covers. I know what makes them sad or scared or happy.

Buildings, trees, and signs zoom by. Then we are underground and I count two more stations: Kenmore, Hynes. The doors slide open, and I step onto the platform of the Copley Square stop. It's crowded and noisy, but I still feel a shiver of excitement.

I am here, I think, *by myself.*

I climb quickly up the dark stairs from underground, with its stinky smells and hissing subway cars, and cross the street onto the plaza. I greet the two large statues of draped women sitting in long skirts outside the library: *Art,* holding a paintbrush, and *Science,* holding the world.

In no time I am up the stairs and through the doors. Inside, I walk lightly on the pink marble, say hello to the lions, as silent as stones. At last it is safe to take my earmuffs off.

The first time my parents took me to the Boston Public Library, I was four and crying from subway screeches, trucks, car horns, loud-talking people, wind blasting around skyscrapers. We stepped through the revolving door into the marble lobby, and whoosh, the silence stopped my tears.

"Welcome to the BPL," Mom said.

"Welcome to the quietest place we know," Dad

whispered, and lifted me up to touch the lion.

I touch the lion's paw again today, as I do every time. I go upstairs, through the old building and its room full of lamp-lit tables and people softly turning pages or asking hushed research questions, reading glasses on noses. I enter the bright Johnson Building, pass by the marble drinking fountains, and walk into the purple-paned children's section.

I work my way down the just-my-height shelves, through the alphabet—Alexander, Blume, Choldenko, DiCamillo—until a new spine attracts me and I pull it out. I read the description and the first sentence or two. When I meet characters I can't wait to get to know, I stack their stories in my arms, take my pile, and fall into one of the comfy chairs.

The library is perfect. There are no other sounds but words heard between my ears. I read about Raymie straight through without stopping. Her story makes me sigh and ache in a good way. Sometimes a book is so good, I want to tell someone right away.

I close the cover and look up. The librarian is at her computer. Two little kids chase each other by the lion cub model, annoying an older boy doing homework. A babysitter reads books to a squirmy child. No one looks at me.

Deb and I used to talk about books. Not now. I no longer want to be her backup friend or part of the flute-playing girls. Maybe fifth grade will be the year of earmuffs and the second year without a friend who is not a fish or in a book.

The thought of no more Ms. Min, or Deb-and-Kiki, or Lina's perfect high notes makes me happy. But if I quit flute, I'll have to find a music class that works for me. I don't want to go to Mr. Skerritt again. Trumpet and trombone are the only choices left.

I think of Madge then, and how she didn't choose flute like all the other girls. On the library computer, I search the catalog for books about girls and trombones. There's a story called *Little Melba and Her Big Trombone*, and the library has it. And even though it's a picture book for little kids, I read it from cover to cover, including the notes at the end.

Melba Liston was not shy. At seven, she began playing the trombone, and when she was grown, she played jazz in bands that had never allowed a woman trombonist to perform with them before.

Melba reminds me of Madge, the way she asks questions and doesn't do what's expected either. I add the book to my pile to take home.

"Find everything you wanted?" the librarian at checkout asks me.

"Yes." I hold up Raymie's book after she scans it. "This story is great. It's about a girl who wants to win a competition and saves a dog and makes two friends—"

The phone rings. "Excuse me," the librarian says. She continues checking out my books while she tells the person on the phone about how to rent a movie from the library online.

I put my books in my backpack after they've been scanned. She's still talking. There's no reason for me to stand there anymore. And anyway, I am not brave like Raymie. Or Melba.

I place my earmuffs on and walk to the outbound station entrance to take me home. At the bottom of the stairs I hear a sound—a soothing horn sound echoing off the station walls. The melody lifts me even though it is blue and slow, like the mourning dove's call that Dad and I heard once.

I stop and stare. It's a girl playing a trombone, like Melba. She is older than a teenager and yet not quite grown-up. She's gliding the slide down like her arm is part of the brass, her lips flat against the mouthpiece. Even though she's making music and can't talk, her eyes are welcoming.

I find a quarter in my backpack and drop it into her open case.

She finishes her song, wets her lips, and grins. "Thanks."

Before I lose my nerve, I say in a rush: "Only one girl at my school plays trombone." I add, "I chose flute, but I think I made a mistake."

"T-bone is the best!" The girl raises her horn, and before she starts again, she says, "It's great to practice with a friend."

I nod. I want to ask her more—when did she start and how many girl trombone players does she know and has she ever heard of Melba—but my train arrives, and suddenly the station is too loud.

I adjust my earmuffs so my ears are completely covered, and find a seat. My backpack is heavy with books. My CharlieCard is in my pocket. In the darkness between stations, I catalog the trip—lion's paw, new books, time in the comfy chair. Somehow I feel a little empty. I turn to the sureness of math. I count the windows as we emerge from underground: *seven windows times two sides times five-car train is seventy windows.*

The multiplication helps a little, but the sad horn song sticks in my head. If I quit flute, maybe I should try trombone, even if that means being in the same class with too-loud Madge. Trees, buildings, cars blur by outside the subway window. I remember it was Madge who gave me back my book. And Madge who tried to apologize for Noah's trumpet joke. Maybe trombone players are nice, like the girl in the station, like Melba. Like Madge.

The subway stops at my station, and I get off alone. I tap my CharlieCard and pass through the turnstile like a marathon winner, hands raised. I look around to see if anyone notices, and my excitement fades. I did it—I made the trip by myself—but there's no one to share it with.

CHAPTER 8

On Sunday, in the middle of page ninety-two of my new book, the doorbell rings unexpectedly.

It makes me jump. Dad too. We're both sitting on the sofa. He gives me a quick reassuring smile. Mom goes to answer the door.

"Hi, Sue!" she says, greeting Deb's mom.

"Do you have two eggs we can borrow?" Sue asks. "We're making muffins, and we're out."

"Of course!" Mom leads Sue into the kitchen, the two of them chattering.

Dad folds the newspaper on his lap and closes his eyes. I can tell he's waiting for their conversation to end, because there is no concentrating on anything until it's over.

I flip a few pages in my book. I can't read either, so I might as well listen. It's impossible not to listen, anyway.

"I heard Amelia's in flute class now! How great." Deb's mom sounds like a TV announcer, cheerful even when they don't want to be.

"Yes," Mom says. "We think it's a better fit than choir."

"Deb just loves it. She is such a natural!"

Guilt rushes through me. I haven't told Mom and Dad that I want to quit flute, and now Sue and Mom are talking about music class.

The two return from the kitchen and stand in the living room. Mom hands her a plastic container with two eggs snug inside so they don't break. "Maybe Deb and Amelia can practice together," Mom says.

"I heard they already did, after school last week." Deb's mom glances in my direction. I look down quickly at my page again. The words float meaninglessly.

"Oh, that's wonderful." I can sense that Mom is looking at me too. "Amelia didn't mention it."

I keep pretending that I'm reading. Deb and I

will not practice together again, but I can't say that without admitting my plan to quit the flute. I wish Mom and Sue would hurry up and finish talking so I can go back to my book.

"I better get back to muffin-making. Before you know it, we'll be carving pumpkins," Sue says. "Deb is going as a princess."

"That's nice," Mom murmurs. "We haven't talked about costumes yet."

The thought of Halloween makes me sink deeper into the sofa. I glance at Dad, who now has his eyes open and is taking deep breaths. He winks and inhales, lifting his hands and dropping them on the exhale. I know he wants me to breathe too. But I don't feel like breathing or counting.

At last, the door closes. Dad breathes out one last time, hugely, and drops his hands dramatically, which makes me giggle.

Mom looks at the two of us. "What?" she says. "Can't I have a friend come over to chat?"

"I didn't say anything," Dad says mildly.

"You could try to be more friendly," she says, "instead of sitting there, making a show of breathing. Both of you."

"It's hard to read when people are talking," I say.

I don't know why she is impatient with us today. We just like quiet more than she does. Is that so hard to understand?

"I needed a break anyway," Dad says. He holds the newspaper up and begins to read again.

Mom heads into the kitchen, muttering, "Most people don't think social visits are interruptions. Most moms don't hear news about their child from someone else."

Dad pats my arm, as if I shouldn't worry about Mom's mood. "Any costume ideas?" he asks.

"I don't know." Last year, my dinosaur tail was trampled by the crowds. And without noise-canceling headphones this year, all the shouting and door-belling will be loud. "Maybe I'm too old for trick-or-treating."

"Better go now before you're a teenager," Dad teases. "I'll help."

I'm not fooled. He always likes an art project. I think some more. The best thing about turning ten has been getting my CharlieCard, and I love the story of Charlie on the T. I say, "What about as a CharlieCard?"

"Yes! I could buy two large poster boards for us to paint." Dad is excited.

I like the idea too. I'll be an original.

• • •

Dinner is soup, and we're so busy slurping and dipping bread that it takes me a while before I notice that Mom is not talking tonight, even when Dad brings up my costume idea. I'm quiet too, thinking about school tomorrow and how I'm going to quit flute.

"I'll let you two tackle the kitchen tonight." Dad excuses himself to go fold the laundry.

Mom begins putting away leftovers. Earmuffs on, I start washing the dishes. They help me concentrate on my thoughts, which are running like water from the faucet.

"It's great you are in flute class with Deb," Mom says, suddenly talkative. "Why didn't you mention that you two are practicing together?"

I wipe away soup on the inside of the pot. "Only once. And Deb is friends with Kiki now."

"Deb can have more than one friend," she says.

"Just because we live in the same building doesn't make us instant friends." Mom is forgetting that Deb and I have only been sort of friends since third grade.

"You can try, Amelia." She hands me the serving bowl to wash. "And it would be nice to hear about it from you instead of from Deb's mom."

Warm water runs over my soapy hands, and I concentrate on cleaning as if that were the most important thing. The truth is, it's impossible to explain why I didn't tell her about practicing with Deb. Mom would first have to understand about Deb-and-Kiki and shrieking flutes and lunch tables.

"Why don't you invite Deb over this week to practice again," Mom says. "And don't wear those earmuffs so much."

I don't answer. I am thinking about cold cheese sandwiches and banana chipmunk cheeks. What if pretending to like an instrument is as bad as pretending to like someone?

Mom stands too close. "Amelia, did you hear me?"

I shift away, placing the last pot into the drying rack.

"Amelia, take off your earmuffs when I am talking to you!" Mom yells right next to my head.

"Stop!" I shout. My wet hands press on my earmuffs.

"What's going on?" Dad appears in the kitchen.

"Mom is bugging me," I say. "And now my fluff is wet."

Mom turns on Dad. "I can't believe you gave Amelia those earmuffs!"

"They're temporary," Dad says in a low voice, but I hear the frustration behind his words.

"Now Amelia has a new fixation," Mom fires back. "Mr. Skerritt said—"

"I am quitting the flute," I announce, desperate to distract them and put an end to their angry voices.

They stop speaking and stare at me.

"Now, Amelia—" Mom says.

"Amelia Mouse—" Dad says at the same time.

"I am *not* a squeaky mouse! And I'm not friends with Deb!" I shake water off, run to my room. I close my door hard. Without slamming.

CHAPTER 9

I'm about to walk out the apartment door for school when Mom puts her hand gently on my shoulder. "Amelia, will you talk to Mr. Fabian today? He needs to know why you're dropping flute."

I nod and squirm away from her touch.

She sighs. "I'm sorry for yelling at you last night. And at Dad, too."

"It's okay," I say, just to get the conversation over.

"No, it's not." Mom exhales. "I am trying to help you, to understand you."

I feel a little guilty now for ignoring her soft knock on my bedroom door last night. But I wasn't ready to talk. I take a slow breath and try to explain now. "I need my earmuffs, Mom."

"I see that. But remember when we talked to Mr. Skerritt? We agreed you'd try to adjust to sounds, to learn music."

"I *am* trying!"

"I know. I want you to be happy." She pulls me in for a hug. "So why are you quitting flute?"

I relax into her arms, searching for a way to explain without mentioning Deb-and-Kiki. "The flutes are too high-pitched. I like the low sound of the trombone."

"All right, but no more switching instruments after this." She gives me one more squeeze. "When you don't wear your earmuffs all day, I'll be so proud of you."

I twist away and put on my backpack. In the hall, I push the down elevator button, jam on my earmuffs. Mom doesn't understand at all. My earmuffs are the only thing saving me from all the everyday sounds bombarding my ears.

As soon as I walk into room twelve, and before it gets too crowded, I stand in front of Mr. Fabian's desk. I slide my earmuffs down, and he smiles kindly at me.

"How are you doing, Amelia?"

It's hard to get the words out, but I know it's the

right decision. "Flute is not for me. When I blow into it, it shrieks." *Like Kiki*, I think.

"It takes practice, Amelia." His cheerful tone is gone.

I take a deep breath. And remind myself I don't want to go to counseling anymore.

"I'd like to try trombone," I say. Maybe he will break the news to Ms. Parker.

I hear the clumping of shoes, the thumping of backpacks on the floor, the screeching of chairs as the room starts to fill behind me.

His lips press into a thin line, the opposite of the *O* that Ms. Min has been showing us in class. "Please see Ms. Parker after school."

My heart sinks like a low note. Mr. Fabian understands why music is so hard for me, but will Ms. Parker? I reposition my earmuffs over my ears.

"Amelia's in trouble!" Noah yells.

"Amelia's in trouble!" Lina repeats.

"Amelia's in trouble!" Kiki loud-whispers to Deb.

The word "trouble" drums on my ears, even with my earmuffs on. I take my seat. Mr. Fabian snaps and claps, and everyone stops talking during silent reading. I am still not listening as he starts on math. My chest feels as tight as my earmuffs' band. *Two pencils on every desk is forty-two pencils in our classroom. Three bookshelves with five rows each is fifteen rows of books.*

I don't look at Jax or Madge or anyone. The numbers, neat and clear, shuttle back and forth between my earmuffs.

Mr. Fabian is talking about different numbers, though. "You all know the answer to three plus one," he says, and Ryan shouts out "Four!"

"Right!" Mr. Fabian grins. "Now watch." He writes three plus one times five on the board. "How do we simplify this mathematical expression?"

I see the problem: Is the answer twenty or eight? I get twenty when I add three plus one, which is four, and multiply four times five. But if I multiply five by one and then add in the three, I get eight.

Mr. Fabian writes on the board: *Multiplication and Division are always evaluated before Addition and Subtraction.* He underlines the first letter of some of the words.

"I'll never remember that," Madge complains.

Mr. Fabian taps each underlined letter. "Just say 'My Dear Aunt Sal' in your head, and you will always know."

"I *do* have an aunt Sally," Madge says, amazed. Which makes everyone laugh, even me.

. . .

As soon as I'm done eating alone, I head to my tube tunnel, curl against the plastic, and quiet my mind. *My Dear Aunt Sal, multiplication and division, then addition and subtraction.* I memorize it.

Math is so much easier than music. And people. I imagine what I am going to say to Ms. Parker at the end of the day. Choir wasn't right for me. Flute isn't either. Will she believe me when I say I tried to make it work? And will trombone be better?

I remember the jazzy horn sound I heard in the subway station. I wonder if Madge would like to hear about that girl trombonist or read the book about Melba who was the first woman to play in an all-man band—

BLAM, BLAM, BLAM, BROING, BROING.

Someone pounds on my tube. Vibrations course through me like electricity. My shoulders hunch, hands instantly land on muffs. I shut my eyes, shutting out, shutting down. I curl up like a mouse—don't move, don't make a noise—and wait for the echoes to die.

Noah pokes his head into the tunnel. Laughing, he says, "Sorry. Did I wake you?"

"Amelia got drummed!" Tyler shouts.

"Go away!" I say, but I don't wait. I scramble down and out the other end of my tube tunnel. I crush maple leaves underfoot all the way to the wall separating school from the street. Breathing hard, I slam into it, like it's home plate. I run my hands along the wall's rough grooves. I am boxed in like the bricks.

My heart hurts as much as my head. I lean against the wall, wishing I could go somewhere in case I cry.

That's when I notice a crate, a stepping stone to the top of the wall. I run over to it, climb up, and look over the playground wall.

It would be easy to drop down on the other side, to run away. Or go up, into the tall pine tree on the other side of the wall.

I decide in a snap and reach for the branches, which are rough on my hands. Sap globs where needles grow. Up and up I go, four, five, six branches, and I've never seen the sky so blue, blue between green needles, hiding me.

I find a safe spot to sit on a thick branch. Slowly, slowly I hear the creak of bending tree, the whisper of needles. A breeze arrives, blowing away mean words, drying my cheeks. I have found a new refuge.

My heart calms. I slide my earmuffs off, let them hang around my neck like a scarf, and I listen to this tree, to me. How can I be me in a loud world? Mom doesn't understand how hard it is. Now Mom and Dad are yelling at each other too, because of me. Because of my sensitive ears.

The lovely quiet is suddenly too quiet. Where are all the shouts and thumping balls and squeaking swings?

The playground is empty. Recess is over. I am in big trouble.

I climb down fast, drop to the crate by the wall, race across the mulch, through the doors opened by the janitor, who lets them slam behind me.

I am late.

Mr. Fabian is already writing spelling words on the board.

"Glad you could join us," he says. "This is your first tardy warning, Amelia."

Trembling, hot-faced, I put my earmuffs on and take a seat. Sounds and thoughts crash inside my head. I hate making Mr. Fabian mad. I wish my muffs could cover up more than ears, could cover up all of me.

When the day finally ends, I walk into Ms. Parker's classroom. I slip my earmuffs off, nervous. No one else has tried three different music classes.

I place the small black case snapped shut onto her desk.

Her face is stern. Even her wild hair droops. "Amelia, Mr. Fabian told me you don't want to play flute, either."

My ears are tingly and sweaty. Will I somehow have to explain what I hear in my head? Music is not melodic to me. It's no earmuffs and no mistakes allowed, and Noah drumming everything.

"You still need to learn music," Ms. Parker says. Then her expression softens. "Let's figure out how."

Relief eases out like a breath. Ms. Parker is going to help. The instrument closet door is open, and I can see all the cases on the shelves. I've tried choir. I've tried flute. It's the last chance to get this right.

I think about Madge and the way she makes people laugh, and Melba and the subway performer. "Trombone," I say.

"Great!" She pulls down a banged-up case and puts the instrument together. "You'll like this." She sticks a funny plunger into the end of the horn. When she blows on the mouthpiece, the sound comes out hushed, like a whisper in a library.

"What is that?" I ask.

"A mute," she says, "for when the trombone goes soft in the background."

I put my hand on the bell and feel its curve. "Trombone will be perfect."

"I hear you're good at math," she says. "That's a great skill for a musician."

"Why?"

"Counting beats in notes, keeping time." Ms. Parker taps her desk. "I'll ask Mr. Fabian to let you come early to class tomorrow. And no more switching instruments after this, okay, Amelia?"

"I promise," I say. And I mean it. This noise-making trombone somehow needs to become my friend.

CHAPTER 10

The next day, I enter the music room noise-lessly. I finger the fluff over my ears, glad to be here before anyone else. All through silent reading and Mr. Fabian talking on and on I worried about how behind I am.

"Come in!" Ms. Parker says, and hands me a long instrument case. "This will be your trombone."

I slip my earmuffs down. The case is worn inside, and the brass has a few dings in it. I twist the pieces together, reminding myself to be grateful to have a free trombone.

"Make your left hand into the letter *L*," Ms. Parker says. She shows me how to hold the trombone. "With your other hand, don't grab the instrument. Use your first two fingers to make a mouth with your thumb around the slide."

It's hard to place my hands just right. She shows me the basic positions of the slide. Nothing is precise.

"How will I ever remember?" I say.

"You'll hear when the note is right." Ms. Parker smiles at me.

I touch my exposed ears. Will they help me for once? I hope she's right.

The door opens and the others arrive, including Madge, all talking, and putting together their instruments. Ms. Parker tells everyone I'm in the trombone class now. There are six of us, four boys and two girls—Madge, and now me.

"Hooray!" Madge takes the chair next to me, taps her foot, and buzzes into her mouthpiece. "I'm warming up my lips," she says.

My earmuffs go up over my ears. I wiggle the slide up and down.

"Okay, let's start," Ms. Parker says. "Don't puff out your cheeks. Pretend you're sucking a lemon—this is called embouchure." She pulls her lips into a weird expression. "Give me your best sour faces!"

And we all do. Madge plays three notes in a row, like she's laughing through the instrument.

I press my lips flat on the cold mouthpiece and blow softly—not enough, and the note leaks out, like a tire deflating. I inhale deeply, blow more air.

I am surprised—the sound from the end of the horn is sweet. My tone isn't brassy. It's not scratchy or sharp. It's a round sound, a warm embrace, not shrill like a flute.

It's the first sound I've liked in a long, long time.

"That's good!" Ms. Parker beams at me. "All together now."

We play "London Bridge Is Falling Down," me for the first time, fumbling to follow Madge's slide positions.

Tyler gets frustrated. "Where's E again?" he asks.

Madge moves his hand lower on the slide. "Second position, there," she says. And they blow together until they are in tune. I join in at the end, wiggling my slide until my tone matches too.

We play the piece again, and when the school heaters stop banging and all the *toots* and random *blats* come together, it sounds all right.

Just as I get used to the idea of making music, Ms. Parker hands out a new piece. "Great job today, musicians!" she says. "Now we're going to learn 'A Song of Peace' for our fifth-grade holiday concert for the whole school and your parents."

My hand goes up, and I speak before she calls on me: "Onstage, with everybody listening?"

"Just the trombones?" Madge asks.

"Each instrument class will play one piece, and the choir will sing," Ms. Parker explains. "Then we will perform 'A Song of Peace' together."

Madge jumps up and toots her horn, which makes me fold up like a paper bag. My ears sweat under my muffs. I don't want to play in front of anyone.

"Time for new spelling words!" Mr. Fabian is too cheerful after lunch. He hands out black-and-white maps of the United States. "We're going to learn all the state capitals."

"Fifty words?" Noah complains. "That's too many to memorize!"

Fifty divided by two is twenty-five, I think. "Can we do it in two parts?" I ask.

"We'll begin geographically," Mr. Fabian reassures us. "Everything west of the Mississippi first." He shows us where to darken the path of the river on our maps.

I count quickly. That's twenty-four states. Then I notice a pattern: Atlanta, Augusta, Austin, Annapolis, Albany all start with *A*.

"What's the capital of Nebraska?" Jax asks Madge.

"How should I know," she says.

Jax shouts, "Oma-ha!"

"It's Lincoln," I say.

Jax isn't listening. "Oma. Get it? Remember when she made pie and I ate and ate?"

Madge laughs. "Makes me hungry for Halloween candy."

"We'll see who gets the most." Jax swings an imaginary bat. "I'm going to be a Red Sox player."

"I'm dressing up as a musician," Madge says.

I circle all the capitals that start with *B*: Boise, Baton Rouge, Bismarck, and of course Boston. Jax and Madge don't ask me what I'm going to be for Halloween. Dad says he will bring home poster board today, and we'll paint it. We'll make a sandwich board for me to wear—one poster board in front, one in back—with straps to hang them from my shoulders. It's going to be awesome. I look over at Madge and Jax. I wish they would ask me, so I can say I'm not telling. That it's a surprise.

Before the bell rings, Mr. Fabian passes out math worksheets. "Tonight's homework is a new challenge," he says.

Instead of all number equations, the problems have the letter *X* where a number should go.

"What does the *X* stand for?" Madge asks.

Deb-and-Kiki eye-roll.

"That's what we will find out." Mr. Fabian doesn't think her question is silly. "It's a puzzle."

I notice that Madge says what she wants, without worrying what Deb-and-Kiki think. She jokes with Jax and knows how to play trombone. And even though Madge's shoelace charms *clink-clank-plink* annoyingly and her voice is loud, I wonder if I could be a bit more like Madge. Not the not-liking-math part. Just the making-friends part.

I am thirty sidewalk lines away from school when I remember I have to bring home my trombone every night. I turn around. By the time I start walking home the second time, it's raining. The trombone is heavy, and the case bangs against my legs. *Step-bump, step-thump.*

I walk slowly, shoulders drooping, earmuffs on, blocking the noise of tires turning on wet streets, like a washing machine. My *step-bump*ing is a steady beat in my ears, and I hope that Ms. Parker is right about counting and playing.

I pull open the lobby door of our building, push the up elevator button, and watch the slow numbers descend—seven, six, five, four . . .

I hear voices singing "Take Me Out to the Ball Game." The door slides open. It is Jax with Deb.

"What are you doing in our building?" I ask Jax.

"Singing!" Jax says, and skips out into the lobby. "What's wrong with that?"

"Nothing." My earmuffs are wet, and I drip onto the floor.

"I forgot, you don't like singing." Jax adjusts his baseball cap, and I brace myself as he opens the lobby door again, letting in cold and rain and noise until the door closes behind him.

Deb holds the elevator open. "Are you coming?"

I shake my head, pointing at my trombone as if there's not enough room in the elevator for me and my case.

She shrugs and lets the door close.

I wait for the next one. *I do like singing*, I should have said to Jax. Just not choir. And even though I'd rather take the elevator by myself, it occurs to me that you can't have a conversation about math expressions or state capitals or trombone positions with friends in books.

As soon as I'm inside our apartment, I carefully put my earmuffs on the radiator to dry. I drop my trombone case in the middle of the living room. I shake fish food into Finway's bowl, and we eat together, Finway gulping and me munching crackers.

"Time to practice," I tell him.

Ms. Parker expects us to practice twenty minutes times five days each week and prove it with a signed-by-a-parent sheet marked with *X*s for every day we play. Take off the zero, and two times five equals ten. Put the zero back on, and twenty minutes times five days equals one hundred minutes. I have to catch up to Tyler and Madge and all the other trombone players.

I cover Finway's bowl with his night cloth to protect him from my playing, and set up my trombone. I make sour lips and hold the trombone up, slide in position. *F*, I think. I blow. That is the first note, first position. It sounds all right.

I hold the note to practice my long tones. I wiggle until I find E in second position the way

Madge showed Tyler today, and blow, then return to first position for F. I hold the note, then glide to third for E-flat, which is easy, and then slide back fast to first for F. Next I play D in fourth position, holding my tone, before returning to F.

I rest my trombone on the floor. I'm dizzy from blowing and my lips hurt. How will I ever remember all the positions? When will it sound like music? I feel like Finway, swimming without getting anywhere.

After dinner, Dad spreads newspaper all over the floor. He lays down the two poster boards, and we get to work.

I draw the subway windows on the back. Dad helps with Charlie on the front, sketching him with his hat sideways. When Dad is done, I paint the words "CharlieCard" in black and green.

From old magazines, I cut out pictures of people waving. I glue them onto the back, so it looks like they are waving from the subway window.

"It looks wonderful," Mom says.

And it does. It will be the coolest costume ever. The only problem is, who will I go trick-or-treating with this year? Last year, I trailed behind Deb-and-Kiki. I'm not doing that again.

"Let's play checkers while it's drying," Dad says.

I sit down opposite him, my now dry earmuffs around my neck. Dad is black; I am red. He moves a piece on the board.

"How was music class today with Ms. Parker?" he asks.

I move one of my checkers diagonally. "I like the sound of the trombone, especially when it's only me playing."

We play without talking, taking turns, trying to outwit each other. I make one bad move, and Dad jumps over three of mine.

He watches me. "Amelia, are you taking breaks from earmuff-wearing?"

I don't answer. We were having so much fun, and now he's ruining it. I make another move. Dad pushes a checker close to mine, and I'm trapped.

He leans forward. "Mom and I talked about this. About you trying."

My checkers are surrounded. "I quit." I slide my earmuffs up, even though our home is quiet. "I don't want to play anymore."

"Already?" Dad touches the fluff over my ears. "Maybe these were a mistake." His voice is soft, as if he's apologizing.

I pull back, out of reach. That's the same thing Mom said. "They are not a mistake." I start putting the game away.

"I know it's hard," he says. "Focusing on one thing helps. Pretend Mr. Fabian's words are birds to find."

He's speaking so calmly that we don't notice Mom standing in the doorway until she speaks.

"Amelia, take those off," she says sharply. "They need to be washed."

Dad's shoulders rise, as do mine. To us, Mom's voice is loud. *Too* loud.

"There's no need to shout," Dad says. "I'm handling this. Amelia and I were talking—"

"Don't you see what's happening?" Mom isn't quiet. "We agreed—" She interrupts herself and turns to me. "Amelia, let me wash them and you can take a break, just for a day or two, while they dry."

"No." I don't want to give Mom my earmuffs. She will ruin them in the washer. And I do not want to go without earmuffs, not even for a day.

"You can't use them to hide." Mom's voice rises more.

I stand up. "We're talking about *my* ears," I say. "And *my* earmuffs. I'll take care of them."

Mom and Dad stare at me, as if I am a different person.

I turn on Dad. "You should understand. I can't believe you're taking her side! And, Mom, you don't know what it's like to be me!"

I fly to my room. Our apartment feels too small to contain the three of us. They can't stop me from handling fifth grade the way I planned. I slide down my muffs, press my ear against my closed door. Mom's and Dad's voices continue. They are not inside voices. I hold my breath and listen.

"She's right," Dad is saying. "You don't understand."

"No, I don't. But I'm trying to help our daughter. She has no friends."

"That's not true—"

"You're not paying attention, then."

I put my earmuffs back on to block them out.

Two parents plus one is three.

Three minus one is two.

Two minus one is one.

Me, always alone. I rest one muffed ear on my shoulder. Sometimes I wish I could change how I am.

CHAPTER 11

Breakfast is extra quiet. I butter toast, scraping the knife softly. Dad drinks coffee without slurping. I put my empty plate in the dishwasher. Mom doesn't talk while making sandwiches. I drop my lunch bag into my backpack, put on my coat and earmuffs, and start for the door.

"Wait, Amelia." Mom reaches for her coat. "I've rearranged my schedule so I can walk to school with you today."

"I don't think she needs—" Dad starts.

"I'd like to, though." Mom is serious. And for once, she doesn't say anything about my earmuffs.

I keep my mouth shut, not wanting to side with either Mom or Dad.

Outside, I start counting lines immediately, but I'm interrupted.

"The only time we get to talk is walking," Mom says. "Your costume looks great. You and Dad are so creative."

"Thanks." I relax my shoulders. Maybe Mom and Dad aren't still mad at each other.

Mom matches her steps with mine. "Sue mentioned Deb is going trick-or-treating in Kiki's neighborhood this year."

I am not surprised. "Deb-and-Kiki are both dressing up as princesses," I say.

"Who will you go trick-or-treating with?"

I frown. I don't want to talk about Halloween. "Maybe Jax?" I say. But I know he will go with his brothers.

"Do you want to ask someone else?" Mom asks. "Maybe from trombone class?"

"Madge is loud," I say. A light turns green, and cars roar through the intersection. I press against my earmuffs until the noise lessens, twenty steps later.

Mom touches my muffed ears. "You know, the only reason I suggest less earmuff time is so you can make friends." Her voice is extra quiet.

I jerk away. "I am trying."

I concentrate on my feet, moving me closer to school. When I was little, Mom used to point out patterns in the subway stations, the petal-like clusters of white tiles, six around one black. *How many altogether?* she would ask. I counted ten black tiles, and I knew the answer: seventy tiles on the platform. Mom always cheered. Now the thing Mom wants most from me I can't do—I can't go through the day earmuff-less.

At last we reach the intersection by school. "I'll go trick-or-treating with you," she says in a bright voice. "We'll have fun, okay?"

"Mom. I'm ten," I say. But I'm a tiny bit glad. I won't be completely alone on Halloween.

"Let's divide some numbers!" Mr. Fabian says, as if everyone will cheer. He hands out division worksheets with long lines of problems. The first one is: divide four hundred and eighty by six.

I hear the times table between my ears: *Four times thirteen is fifty-two, like four suits in a deck of cards. Eight times twelve equals ninety-six.* I write answers in the boxes, numbers marching easily down the side of my worksheet.

"You are doing it all wrong," Kiki says in a fake

loud whisper. She isn't looking at me; she's pointing at Madge's page. "Madge wrote letters instead of numbers in the answer boxes."

Deb laughs. Noah says, "This isn't spelling!"

Mr. Fabian claps and snaps, and half the class joins him and shuts up, but it's too late. Madge's face is fall-leaf red. And my shoulders are up around my ears.

I turn my head sideways and read the letters Madge wrote in the boxes where numbers should be: *egdam setah htam.*

"Mind your own business!" Madge places her hands over her page so I can't see.

I am impressed. It's a special talent to be able to write backward. I tear a page out of my notebook and write: *Ikik si naem.*

Madge sees, reads backward, and smiles.

I crumple up the note fast. I didn't know Madge likes to write backward like me, and what does it mean that we both can read backward? If only figuring that out were as easy as dividing.

Over the next few weeks, I sometimes catch Madge backward writing again in class. I continue to wear my earmuffs during school each day. But by the time it's nearly Halloween, everyone's excitement makes school even louder than usual. Mr. Fabian notices too. He seems glad to excuse us for music.

I sit next to Madge in trombone class. The floor by my chair is wet and gross. We have rags to catch the spit blown out the valve at the bottom of the slide, but I miss half the time.

We play through "London Bridge," and it sounds like Madge is the only one playing the right notes. My lips buzz. The sound I make is croaky like a frog. And even with my earmuffs on, all the trombones are like car horns blaring at once.

I raise my hand and ask, "Can we play with mutes today?"

"Sure, let's try," Ms. Parker says, as if she's happy to change the volume too. She gives each of us one.

"Why is it called a mute?" Madge asks, balancing the pointy-hat piece on her head, making everyone giggle. Me too.

"That's a good question," Ms. Parker says. "A mute on a computer or phone means no sound at all." She puts the mute inside the trombone and says, "In a trombone, the mute makes the sound quieter."

Like earmuffs, I think, and Ms. Parker has us all play a scale together. When we blow the notes through the mutes in our trombone bells, the sound is rounded, soft and muffled, as if underwater. It's beautiful.

"I'll find a piece of music that calls for mutes," Ms. Parker says. "For now, let's put them away."

Next we start on "Jingle Bell Boogie," a new song. The sounds Madge makes through her horn are smooth. She glides down and hits all the right notes. She's as tall as a trombone, and her hand holds the slide easily. My slide is all over the place.

At the end, Ms. Parker claps lightly. "Good job sight-reading!" she says. "We'll play this piece in the fifth-grade concert."

My stomach squeezes a little. "What if I make a mistake?"

"That's why we practice." She starts reviewing the tricky parts.

I look at the floor, not listening. I can picture it: the gym packed with chairs, people chatting, shuffling, clapping. And every fifth grader singing, tooting, blaring, and blasting sounds to the ceiling. The concert will be terrible. Trombone is hard, but it's my third and final choice. If I give up on music, though, I'd have to go back to Mr. Skerritt. I take a deep breath and refocus on making no mistakes and not worrying about the concert.

"Bells up," Ms. Parker directs, and I get the very first note wrong. Madge pokes my leg with her slide, and I jump.

"What?" I ask.

Madge surprises me, again. "You'll get it," she says, and smiles.

Practicing is more fun with a friend, I remember the subway trombonist said. But before I think of something nice to say to Madge, the bell rings and she packs her trombone away.

I head straight to my table. I am fine eating lunch alone, but today my cold cheese sandwich sticks a little to the roof of my mouth. I wonder if Madge feels as sad as I do when Kiki is mean. From across the tables, though, I see Madge laughing at something Jax does. My ears are sweaty and itchy. I want to hear what's so funny, but I would have to walk over and drop my earmuffs. Maybe Mom is right and I should try . . . but I just can't.

Outside, I curl in the curve of the tube tunnel, on cold plastic, eyes closed, cocooned and forgotten. *Deb-and-Kiki plus Emma and Lina equals four friends. Jax plus Madge plus Noah equals three friends.* I am not part of the fifth-grade friend equation.

The sounds of swings, running feet, and games rebound against the playground walls and funnel into my tube. Earmuffs are not enough to shut out the fun I am missing.

At the end of the day, I put on my backpack and lift up the trombone case. Its heaviness still surprises me. The case bangs against my legs, through the doors. I stop at the top of the school steps and put the case down to rest.

"You're in the way," I hear Kiki say, even with my muffs on.

Deb-and-Kiki push past me, swinging little black flute cases, ponytails wagging as they walk. *Better to be a T-bone player,* I think, *than to be like them.*

Before I can move, Madge comes through next, and her trombone case bumps me in the legs. I jump.

"Sorry!" she shouts.

I press my hands to my ears.

Jax is right behind her, carrying a baseball he tosses high and catches in his glove.

"Want to play?" he calls to Madge.

"Sure!" She puts down her trombone with a thump and easily catches the extra glove Jax throws her way.

I sit on my case to watch. Jax tosses her an easy

underhand ball, and Madge catches it with a slap against leather. They do three more, back and forth. Madge never misses. She has a good arm, too.

I clap for her, and Madge bows, noticing me.

She throws the ball back to Jax. "Come play too!"

I shake my head. "I'm not very good."

"So what? Just try." Madge hands me the glove.

I stand ready, the glove in front of me, the way Jax and his brothers always do. I am nervous with Madge watching. Jax says something, and I miss what he says *and* the ball, which rolls under a parked car. I cover my eyes with my arm as if that makes me invisible.

"I'll get it," Jax says. "I have to go anyway."

"Me too." Madge picks up her trombone case. "Oma and I are carving pumpkins today!"

"Sorry." I hand Jax back his glove. It feels like I ruined the fun Jax was having with Madge. I lift up my case and trail behind him as we head down our street. Jax tosses and catches the ball all the way to our apartment buildings. He goes inside his and never looks back.

As I wait for the elevator in my building, I wonder: *Would I have caught that ball if I had taken my earmuffs off?*

Inside the quiet of home, I slump on the sofa and think. I remember the way Kiki waits by the door for Deb, how Mr. Fabian talks with Ms. Parker between classes, how Noah brags to Jax and Madge about what he's got in his lunch, then always shares. And Madge is nice to everyone.

It's easy to watch and never say a word. No one talks to me when I am under my muffs.

I decide to practice. I set up my stand, cover Finway's bowl, and twist together my trombone. I wet my lips and play "Jingle Bell Boogie" and "London Bridge Is Falling Down." I close my eyes like Melba, like Madge, like the girl in the subway station. I sound pretty good.

After the last note, I listen to the silence. No one applauds, because Dad isn't home yet. No one says "We did it," because I am practicing alone.

I uncover Finway. "Did you like my playing?"

I look over at my book on the sofa. "Did you like it, Alanna?"

Of course no one answers. And on Friday, I will probably be the only fifth grader trick-or-treating alone, with my mom.

My stomach sits like a pile of spit at the end of my trombone slide.

CHAPTER 12

Our doorbell starts ringing on Halloween in the middle of dinner, making us hurry. Mom jumps up to hand out candy, and I change into one of Dad's blue button-down shirts to look like Charlie. In the living room, Dad holds up the boards of my CharlieCard costume, and I slide in between. The painted boards hang from my shoulders.

It's dark, and I hear more shouting outside. "Hand me my earmuffs, Dad."

"Are you sure?" Mom asks.

"Of course. Subway conductors need to protect their ears," I say. She knows what I really mean is *I need to protect mine from the extra noise tonight.*

"Have fun, you two." Dad takes over the candy

bowl job and stands at the door. I wish he were coming with me, not Mom. But we made a deal.

It's a cold night, so I'm extra glad for my earmuffs. I stand stiffly, not sure where to go. Mom immediately starts talking with the other parents on the street. They all "ooh" and "aah" over the little kids, who are the only ones besides me wearing homemade costumes—a spray-painted robot, a rabbit with hairband ears, and a dragon with a spiky tail sewed onto her pajamas. Suddenly I am not so sure my costume is great.

"Where to?" Mom asks me at last.

I point to Jax's building. In the lobby, I tell Mom, "Wait here." Maybe Jax hasn't left yet. Maybe I could tag along with him.

I arrive at Jax's door at the same time as the robot, rabbit, and dragon. "Trick or treat!" Their yelling grates. I press on my earmuffs and don't speak.

"Is Jax out with his brothers already?" I ask his mom after she has filled everyone's sacks.

She laughs. "Oh yes! Couldn't hold them back—they went down the street."

"Thank you," I say, and catch up to the little kids, as if I planned to trick-or-treat with them through the rest of the building.

My pillowcase fills with candy, but it turns out it's really hard to walk up and down stairs in my CharlieCard costume. The boards get bumped and bent with every step. I take the elevator back down to the street.

Mom is waiting for me on the sidewalk. "Where to next?" she asks.

"Maybe I'm done." I watch the costumed crowds running up the steps of the next building. Our street echoes with shouting and knocking and ringing. My pillowcase is full enough.

Suddenly two ninjas charge by, knocking me into a tree. "Ow!" I cry out.

"Are you okay?" Mom asks, steadying me. "Oh no, your strap broke."

I blink, pushing away tears. "I want to go home." My costume is ruined. Halloween is ruined.

"Hey, Charlie!"

I turn. It's Madge in a tuxedo and quiet shoes, red mittens stuffed into her pockets and bare hands carrying her trombone. I am surprised to see her alone, with just her grandmother. Mom introduces herself to Oma, who is bundled in a heavy coat.

Madge bends down and picks up something.

It's one of the waving-people photos from the back of my costume. "Here. This fell off."

"It doesn't matter. My costume is wrecked," I say.

"What happened?" Oma inspects my broken strap. She pulls tape and a giant safety pin out of her pocket, and in fifteen seconds, my costume is fixed.

"Oma's always prepared!" Madge says with a grin. "Okay, where do you want to go?"

I glance at Mom, who nods encouragingly. Maybe I should give Halloween another chance, this time with Madge. It's almost like she and I planned to meet up all along. The thought makes me smile. I say, "I just did Jax's building."

"Well, let's go to your building, then!" she says.

We cross the street and head inside. Mom and Oma, Madge's trombone, and my wide poster boards don't fit into the elevator.

Mom laughs and turns to Oma. "Let's let the girls go first. Would you like to come over for a cup of coffee?"

Oma agrees, and Madge and I promise to stay together and meet them back at our apartment.

We take the elevator to the top. As we rise, I wonder why Madge isn't trick-or-treating with someone from school. "Why are you out with your grandmother?"

"Oma worries I'll bring home too much candy," Madge says. "She shouldn't! Tomorrow is All Saints' Day, and Oma will make strudel that is even better than candy. It's a tradition."

"My mom wanted to spend time with me."

"And we've escaped," Madge says with a laugh.

We make a plan. I will knock and say "trick or treat" like a song, and Madge will play it on the trombone—A, A, F—quietly, she says, with a glance at my muffs. And it works. It's not too loud. It's just right.

We go from door to door on the top floor and work our way back down. Everyone says our voice-and-trombone trick or treat sounds great. Soon it feels like the best Halloween ever.

When we reach Deb's, her mom answers.

"Who have we here?" She hands us two pieces of candy each.

"I'm a famous trombonist," Madge says, and blows a note.

"I'm a CharlieCard," I say. *Isn't it obvious*, I want to add.

"How clever," Sue says in that way grown-ups do when they really mean the opposite.

I'm glad Deb isn't here.

"I should have done a simpler costume," I say

after Sue closes the door. I could have dressed up as Melba. Then I wouldn't be walking stiffly around corners.

"No way!" Madge says. "You could never be boring!"

"You're a great musician," I say. "You look—and sound—like a real one."

At last we get to my door. Madge and I do our trick or treat duet, singing and tooting in tune.

The door opens. "I thought I heard a trombone!" Dad plops candy into both of our bags.

"Dad, this is Madge," I say.

"Hello! We've been getting to know your grandmother." He opens the door wide, and we both go in. Oma and Mom are sitting at the table, holding on to mugs, talking in low voices. Dad brings us two cups of hot chocolate.

Madge looks around. "Is it okay to talk?" she whispers.

I slide my earmuffs down. "What?"

"I always thought your house would be like a museum," she explains.

"It is quiet, but not silent," I say. "Talking is allowed."

Madge takes a sip. She is studying my head for so

long, I wonder if something is wrong. I ask, "What are you thinking?"

"Your ears are small and pretty," she says. "And they aren't purple!"

Everyone laughs, and so do I. I've been wearing my earmuffs so much, it's like they are a part of me.

"I mean, I know your ears aren't purple." Madge blushes. "But it's nice to see them."

For the next half hour, Madge and I dump out our candy and swap, lollipops for chocolate bars, peanut butter cups for packs of gum. It's so much easier to talk to her when there aren't any crashing sounds.

When it's time for them to go, I walk Madge and her grandmother to the elevator. "Thanks for trick-or-treating with me," I say to Madge.

"It was fun." Madge pushes the button and adds, "I really liked your costume. It's different in the best way."

A warm feeling fills me that has nothing to do with hot chocolate. "See you Monday," I say, at exactly the same moment Madge says it.

"Jinx," she says.

CHAPTER 13

I walk into room twelve and take a deep breath. Today I will go all day unmuffled.

I thought about my "purple" ears all weekend. At home, without earmuffs, my hair felt light on my head. I liked the sound of "A Song of Peace" when I practiced it. My ears didn't get hot when I did my homework. By Sunday night, I decided I'd make today a no earmuffs day. I wouldn't do it for Mom. Or Dad. Or Mr. Skerritt. I'd do it for me—to hear trombone notes. To catch what Jax tosses my way. To be open to Madge's compliments.

I slide my earmuffs off, zip them into my backpack, and remember Melba and Raymie and being brave.

I sit at my desk and wait for the first bell. I have a plan. When it rings, I hold my book over my head like a tent, with the pages over my ears.

"Hi," I say to Madge when she plops into her chair next to mine. I slide the book off and put it on my desk.

Madge looks at my head. "Did you forget your earmuffs?"

"Yeah, where are your earmuffs?" Deb-and-Kiki ask at the same time.

Before I need to answer, Mr. Fabian swoops in. "Find a book to read," he says to the class, and I send him a grateful glance.

It still is un-silent reading, though. I try to concentrate. My head feels extra light. I rearrange my hair over my ears. I look at the words in my book, but I can't stop hearing pages turning, feet moving, noses sniffling.

I glance at my backpack in the cubby. The urge to get my earmuffs is like a mosquito bite I want to itch. Instead I cross my legs. I finger my pretty ears. I want people to notice me, not purple fluff.

Math is next. We work on multiplying and adding long expressions.

"Here's my long expression," Jax says, and pulls

his chin down and his eyebrows up. Everyone laughs. I have to admit, he's pretty funny.

Mr. Fabian gets us back on track. For a while Dad's counting concentration trick works. There are twenty-one chairs with four legs each, which equals—

"Amelia?"

"Eighty-four!" I say.

Mr. Fabian is puzzled. "Try again. What is two hundred divided by four?"

"It's fifty," Deb says. Noah gives her a high five.

The slapping sound makes me flinch. I was concentrating. Just on the wrong thing. I hide my face, retracing each letter of my name on the top of my page until the letters are dark.

"It's okay," Madge says, smiling at me. "You'll get it right next time."

I nod, but I know I never would have made that mistake if I'd had my earmuffs on.

When the bell sounds after social studies, I scrunch my shoulders up and press one ear into my shirt. Everyone breaks into conversation, sneakers squeaking into the hall. My ears feel bruised.

Music is a little better, and Ms. Parker smiles when she sees that my earmuffs are off. I play the right notes. Our trombone sounds are in sync, and after we make it all the way through "A Song of Peace," I relax into the silence that follows the last note.

Madge catches my eye. "Perfect," she says.

I'm glad my earmuffs are off so I can hear her.

And then the quiet is ruined by blatting, spitting, and cases snapping shut. My shoulders rise to my ears, since my hands are busy packing up as quickly as I can. I don't even realize I am holding my breath until I exhale in the hall. I lean against the wall and remember how easy school was with noise-canceling headphones and earmuffs. But then I wouldn't hear Jax's jokes or Madge's laugh.

In the cafeteria, Madge motions me over, and I decide to join her crowded table. Nothing terrible happens—no spills, no surprise loud noises—yet I still count in my head how many times I chew before my sandwich is gone. Eighteen.

"Ha ha! Dog ate my lunch!" Noah holds up a cartoon his mom put into his lunch. I don't look, because everyone presses in too close and I have to lean away. Jax and Madge burst out laughing. I quick-cover my ears.

When there is a break in the conversation, I think

of something I can share, like Noah, and slip out my CharlieCard. "With this, I can go anywhere," I say.

"Your Halloween costume!" Madge says.

"Where did you get it?" Jax leans close, and Noah looks over too. I shift away again so there's more space.

"My parents gave it to me," I say. "I'm allowed to take the T alone."

"I'd go to a Red Sox game," Jax says.

"I go to the library," I say. "Last time I met—"

"You're lucky," Madge interrupts. "Oma won't let me go anywhere."

"What's the big deal?" Noah says. "Let's play tag."

There is a swell of voices, feet thumping, trays stacking, and trash tumbling as everyone heads outside to run around. I sit with my eyes closed, hands on my ears, until the cafeteria is empty.

Outside, I head straight for my tube tunnel, my footsteps on the ladder a prelude to peace and quiet. *Just five minutes*, I think. That's all I need to recharge by myself in my cocoon.

At the top I stop. Ryan, José, and Tyler are inside. They look at me like I'm intruding. But they are the ones crammed in where they shouldn't be.

"What are you doing in my space?" I say.

"You don't own it," Tyler says. "And you weren't here." They keep talking, without moving, without seeing me anymore even though I am still gripping the tunnel opening.

Without my earmuffs, their voices are amplified. I slowly back down the ladder.

I look around the playground, wondering where to go. It's too cold to climb my pine tree, and last time that was a disaster. *No hiding, Amelia.* I give myself a pep talk. *You can do this.*

Madge is talking to Jayden and Cassie. Slowly I move closer until I am standing outside their circle. They are talking about homework and practicing and TV shows and boots. I try to think what I could say that makes sense in the conversation. I end up deciding against mentioning how many beats (four) are in each measure of "Jingle Bell Boogie," or the types of birds Dad identified (pigeon, chickadee, finch) the other day.

The bell rings. I cover my ears and trudge back inside.

As soon as we are all in our seats, Mr. Fabian begins talking about the Constitutional Convention in Philadelphia. Without my earmuffs, it's impossible not to be distracted by Madge's shoelace chimes jangling every time she moves her feet. Noah is drumming on his textbook pages, rapping like he's Alexander Hamilton. I overhear Deb-and-Kiki whispering about Deb's birthday party.

Everything is too much—the noise and the battle to concentrate make my brain hurt. I rest my head on my hands, eyes closed.

"Stop it!" Noah shouts.

I hear shoving, a scuffle. I cover my whole head with my arms.

A textbook slams shut with a loud bang.

I scream. Which makes Cassie and Lina scream. Mr. Fabian yells "Settle down," but everyone is shouting at Noah. At Ryan. At me.

I slap my hands to my ears. I jump out of my chair, pull open the classroom door. I have to get out now.

I run, my sneakers slapping in the hall. My breathing is too loud. I stop and slide down against the wall. Where am I going? I can't run away from school. I press my hands on my eyes. Tears leak out. I wipe them away. I don't want to cry.

The door to room twelve opens and I hear Mr. Fabian say, "Everybody read for a moment."

And then he's there, by my side. "Are you okay?" He shakes his head. "Silly question."

He hands me a note and a hall pass. "Why don't you visit Mr. Skerritt for the rest of today?"

I look up at him. "Am I in trouble?"

"Absolutely not. I bet he'd like to hear about the hard thing you're doing today."

As I walk to the counselor's office, I'm all jumbled. I don't want to go, but I can't spend one more minute in class without earmuffs.

I knock on the door and open it slowly.

"Amelia!" Mr. Skerritt says. "What a nice surprise. Have a seat." His breath rattles in and out as he reads Mr. Fabian's note.

I sit in the chair. I wish I had asked for my earmuffs before I left.

"Mr. Fabian says you needed a break," Mr. Skerritt says.

I nod. "My earmuffs are in my backpack."

"Why?"

I glare at him. "Isn't that what you wanted?"

"I want to know why *you* decided to not wear them."

All my reasons seem not important anymore. "It doesn't matter. It was a mistake."

Mr. Skerritt pulls out a page from my folder. "The other day, Mr. Fabian told me that you're participating in class, even though you are wearing the earmuffs most days."

I don't answer. In the quiet of his office my ears begin to calm down.

"And Ms. Parker says you are playing trombone. That's wonderful," he says.

For the first time I notice that Mr. Skerritt's eyes are kind.

He nestles the page back into the folder and closes it. "Was there a particular noise today that made you walk out of class?"

"All of it!" I burst out in frustration. What doesn't he understand?

He leans back in his chair. "I like the sound of trombones," he says at last. "Do you?"

He wheezes, waiting for me to speak.

When I don't answer, he slides a piece of paper over. "Can you write down the sounds you like? Good sounds?"

"Not bad ones?" That list would be easy.

"Good ones," he says firmly.

I concentrate and, like a librarian, sort sounds like they're books on shelves. That makes me think of the Boston Public library. And I remember the first note I played. I write down two good sounds:

1. Walking on pink marble
2. Playing trombone by myself

Then I think a little more, and write down:

3. Madge's laugh

Mr. Skerritt leans over. "That's a nice list."

"Now can I make a list of bad sounds?" I ask.

"Well, as long as it doesn't include everything." Mr. Skerritt takes another wheezy breath. "How about writing down only the worst ones. The really annoying sounds."

I look around the room. The poster on the wall reminds me that mistakes mean I am trying. And I *am* trying. I think of all the noises in Mr. Fabian's room, which are mostly manageable sounds. Ms. Parker, too, understands when sounds are sweet or wrong. She makes sure we're in tune. I think some more and write three of the worst sounds:

1. When people hammer on my tunnel
2. When Noah honks his trumpet
3. When Deb-and-Kiki tease

"Hmmm," Mr. Skerritt says. "That's an important list. May I keep it?"

I nod. His breathing rasps as he adds it to my folder. I try not to look at the hairs in his ears. The clock ticks. Soon it will be time for art in room twelve. Maybe I can handle that without earmuffs. "Can I go?"

Mr. Skerritt hands me a note to take back to Mr. Fabian. "I'm proud that you tried going without earmuffs today, Amelia. Even if it was hard."

"Thanks," I mumble. "I didn't make it through the whole day, though."

"That's okay." His ears rise as he smiles. "A whole day is a lot for your first time. You will learn when you need them and when you don't."

I'm out the door. Writing down sounds doesn't really make them bearable. I know the one thing that will, and I can't wait to put them back on.

I peek into Mr. Fabian's room. Everyone is quietly working. I slip in, open my backpack, and take out my earmuffs. I slide them on, and the relief makes me exhale as I sit at my desk.

"Welcome back," Mr. Fabian says quietly to me. "We're making self-portrait collages."

I start cutting out shapes for my head, body, and legs. The sound of chatting, scissors snipping, and glue squirting is back to a five-out-of-ten range.

Noah slides a piece of paper over. "Here's purple," he says.

I look at him, puzzled. And then I get it. Purple for my earmuffs. My face warms, but I don't care.

"Noah!" Madge scolds.

"It's a joke!" he says.

"It's okay," I say, taking the paper. I cut out purple muffs for my collage. It's like Mr. Skerritt said: I can decide. And right now, even my self-portrait wears earmuffs.

Madge gives me a funny glance, but I don't say anything.

At the end of the day, I stand on the school steps. The outside noises of cars pulling up and people yelling "See you tomorrow!" surround me, but I am buffered by earmuffs, an island on the steps. The day has been so horrible, and for what? People still only see purple fluff, not me.

All the way home, I walk two blocks behind Jax and Deb. Even though Mr. Skerritt didn't want me to, I add more to the list of sounds I hate—un-silent reading, trash cans knocked over, flute show-offs.

All through setting the table and making dinner, I'm extra quiet.

When we sit down to eat, Mom notices. "Everything all right?"

I mash potatoes with my fork. "I'm not hungry."

"How was school?" Mom asks.

"Is trombone still better than flute?" Dad asks. "Better than choir?"

I know Dad is trying to point out the bright side, but I glower. "Today was a disaster."

"What do you mean?" Dad asks.

"I did what you said." I glare at Mom, then Dad. I swallow hard, as if all the noises I heard today are going to explode out of me. "I lasted almost all day without earmuffs, even though silent reading was loud, lunch was awful, and recess was worse. It didn't work."

"Oh, Amelia Mouse—" Dad says, at the same time Mom asks, "What happened?"

"Nothing happened!" I shout. "Except Noah slammed shut his textbook and then I screamed and then everyone went crazy and then I was sent to Mr. Skerritt."

Mom and Dad look at each other.

"Was it good to talk to Mr. Skerritt?" Mom asks.

"That's not the point!" I push my chair back and stand. "Everything was too crashing and distracting!

I had to put my earmuffs back on! And the holiday concert is coming soon, and I don't know if I can survive all the fifth graders playing instruments at once!"

I pick up my earmuffs and smash them over my head, hard. "Mom, you can't force me to stop wearing them. And I'll wash them when I'm ready."

I run to my room and slam my door. For the First. Time. Ever.

CHAPTER 14

When I come out of my room the next morning, both Mom and Dad are sitting on the sofa, waiting for me. Losing my temper equals I'm in trouble. I touch my head instinctively, wishing I had my earmuffs on like an invisibility cloak.

"Sit down." Dad pats the seat next to him.

I squish between them. "I'm sorry I slammed my door," I blurt.

"Thank you for saying that," Dad says.

"We understand why you were upset." Mom leans in to give me a hug. "What you did yesterday was brave. You tried going without earmuffs!"

"It didn't work." I cross my arms. "I was counting and concentrating so much that I couldn't pay attention to the right things. I gave the wrong answer in math class."

"That must have been hard," Dad says. "It's okay to make mistakes sometimes. Everyone does."

"We're proud of you." Mom is smiling. "And we'd like to do something fun together, next weekend, as a family."

I can't believe I'm not in trouble. Still, what I really want to do is read all day and not go to school.

"You still have to go to school today," Dad says, as if he is reading my mind. "Where do you want to go on Saturday? Your choice."

I immediately think of the Boston Public Library and its comfy chairs. But that's not the right place. "Can I wear my earmuffs?" I ask.

"You decide," Mom says.

I look outside. Mr. Skerritt said it was okay to experiment. Maybe I can practice going un-muffed with Mom and Dad first, somewhere in between quiet and loud, where noises can float away. "Let's go to Boston Common."

"It's a date," Dad says.

. . .

On Saturday, we walk together to the station. Dad has his binoculars around his neck. I wear my earmuffs on the T. When the track squeals intensify, Dad leans over and says, "How many seats in this car?"

Eight double seats on each side makes sixteen on the left, sixteen on the right. Sixteen times two is thirty-two. I count twenty single seats. "Twenty plus thirty-two is fifty-two seats," I say.

Mom joins in our game. "Of the fifty-two passengers, how many are wearing hats?" she asks.

I count in my head, turning around, even though people give me funny looks. "Twenty-four," I whisper. I know what she's going to ask next. "Fifty-two minus twenty-four is twenty-eight not wearing hats."

"That's my math whiz," Mom says, and gives me a squeeze. "And one girl wearing earmuffs."

I smile. "Twenty-seven, then."

One stop after Copley, we get off at Arlington Station and take the stairs up. I count those, too, until we are out and across the street and in the park.

"Where to?" Dad says.

I slide my muffs down, because it's my choice. And listen. Birds are singing in trees, and people are catching Frisbees, riding bikes, and playing guitars on blankets, even though it's November and chilly.

Mom is silent, but it's a happy quiet. It's like being outside blows away whatever she worries about.

"Let's go over to the duckling statues," I say. I know she will like that; we used to read *Make Way for Ducklings* together. We take a photo of me every year, graduating from one duck to the next, beginning with when Dad balanced me on Quack, the littlest of the eight ducklings. Last year, when I was nine, I sat on Mrs. Mallard.

As usual, there are tons of kids around the statues. We have to wait our turn. Dad has wandered off under the trees, his binoculars pointed up. Mom holds her phone at the ready. I worry about which duck to sit on, who's next, and all the voices trying to get babies to smile at cameras.

BAM!

My hands clap onto my ears, elbows out, and I plow my head into Mom's stomach, as if I'm five again.

"Just a truck backfiring," Mom murmurs, her hands gentle on my hair. I lean into her, push my earmuffs on, and feel safe.

"Poor thing," I hear a woman say loudly. "It must be hard for her, being the way she is."

I snap my head up. The woman is standing next to Mom, talking about *me*. Even though she doesn't know me at all. My reaction to a loud sound *is* part of who I am, the same as loving math and writing backward and re-reading books.

"My daughter is none of your business," Mom says with a bite to her voice.

The woman's lips press into an unfriendly line, and I tug at Mom's arm to leave, so they won't get into an argument. Mom takes my hand in hers, firmly. When we're far enough away from that nosy woman, Mom starts up again.

"People make me so angry! Making assumptions about you and—"

"It's fine, Mom." It's strange to be comforting her; I am the one who deals with people all the time. I wish I could fly like a bird up into a tree, where Dad will find me and take me home.

She hears the quiver in my voice and puts her arm around me. "Are you okay?"

I nod and hold on to her. The terribleness of a sudden sound and mean words makes it hard for me to speak. "I'm sorry I jumped—I'm trying to be better."

"Oh honey." Mom stops and crouches down so

we're eye to eye. "You don't need to apologize."

I blink to stop tears from falling, but a few escape and run down my cheeks. "But you said you'd be proud of me when I go a whole day without ear-muffs, and I failed at school. And today, too . . ." A sob escapes, and now I'm really crying.

"You didn't fail. You tried! Amelia, that makes me so proud," Mom says, pulling me into a crushing embrace. "I'm sorry if I made you think I was dis-appointed in you the other day."

I dry my eyes on my sleeve and give her a half smile. "Maybe we can go somewhere quiet? Like home?"

"Of course." She kisses my head.

"Can I join in on that cozy hug?" Dad says, walk-ing over.

Mom rests her arm on his shoulder. "We're done for today," she says.

"Already?" Dad is surprised. "Did something happen?"

Mom and I look at each other. She lets me decide what to say, which makes me glad. "I've outgrown taking my photo with a duckling. That's all," I say.

CHAPTER 15

Step-thump, step-bump. Sidewalk line eighty. Sixteen more to get to school. It's cold and my earmuffs are on, doing double duty. Keeping me warm and muffling sound. I'm not sure I will ever take them off again.

Even this weekend wasn't a break from mean people.

Mr. Fabian hands back math quizzes. I notice that Madge has a zero on hers. For the first time, she is quiet. Her hands are over *her* ears.

I've never seen her without words. Maybe I can give her some. Backward ones. I rip a little piece of paper and write, *Htam sah skcirt.* I slide it over quietly.

She reads it and looks at me. "What tricks?"

I think of my favorite, easiest one. "What is nine times six?" I ask.

"Fifty-two?" Madge guesses.

I shake my head. "Do you want me to show you?"

She folds over her math quiz. "Anything would be better than this."

"It's easy," I say. "The two digits of every nine times table add together to equal nine. See? Fifty-four is five and four, and added they make nine."

Madge's face is scrunched up. "I don't get it."

"Nine times nine is eighty-one." I write an eight and a one on the page. "Eight plus one equals nine."

"You're lucky you're good at math," she says.

"You are better at music. You hit all the notes right."

"True!" Madge watches while I write down nine times four equals thirty-six. "Three plus six is nine!" Her laugh, which is wonderful, is now number one on my list of good sounds.

At lunchtime, I stand next to Madge. I decide to try joining her table again, this time with my earmuffs on. "Can I eat with you guys today?"

I am holding tight to my brown-bag lunch. I am holding my breath in too.

"Sure," Madge says.

This time, adding myself in at the table feels as easy as one plus three. I sit between Madge and Jax. Noah sits opposite. Jax is telling a story about Mookie Betts and the Red Sox, but I also hear Madge's shoe chimes jingling, Kiki's voice across the room, and the doors swinging.

My shoulders hunch, and I focus on my sandwich. I imagine the holiday show and the combined music rehearsal and everyone all together—it'll be even louder than this. My ears sweat under my muffs.

Madge pokes me.

"What?" I look up. Deb-and-Kiki are standing next to our table.

"Here's an invitation to my birthday party next month," Deb says, handing me an envelope.

"Her mom made her invite everyone in our class," Kiki adds, giving an invitation to Madge, too.

"Where's mine, then?" Jax asks.

"Just girls," Kiki says, as if that should be obvious.

"Awww," Noah says, but Deb-and-Kiki are gone.

I shove the envelope into my lunch bag. I hate parties, especially the kind where you had to be invited.

"At least we can go together," Madge says, shrugging. "Let's go outside."

On the playground, Madge runs to join a game of tag. The chill makes me shiver. It's like opening our lobby door, the cold air prodding me to move.

"I'm in too," I call out. I run under the monkey bars, past the swings, by my tube tunnel. Without my old headphones I feel light, fast. Breathless, I lean against the familiar plastic.

Tyler is it, and after a moment I realize that he isn't chasing me. Without a second thought, I climb into the tube for a break. The cold, the curve, the quiet—I exhale. My breathing slows. Running is nice but so is sitting in the tube. Can I be someone who needs quiet *and* eats at Madge's table *and* plays tag with everyone?

November has brought even colder weather, and now our cubbies are jammed with scarves, hats, and heavy coats. On the way to the full fifth-grade rehearsal, I count the cubbies. Eight, two rows high on both walls from Mr. Fabian's to the music room. *Eight and eight make sixteen. Sixteen times two walls is thirty-two cubbies.*

Ms. Parker's music room is already crowded when I arrive. Everyone is putting together instruments and blowing through mouthpieces. I find a space where I can get my trombone ready.

As I stand there, earmuffs on, Ms. Parker pulls me aside. "What do you think about trying no earmuffs? You did it once."

"Okay." I bravely slide down my earmuffs, even though I want to say that day was terrible.

"Good," she says. "I'll help. You'll see."

I don't know what she thinks she can do. Still, I sit down next to Madge and wait with my ears exposed.

"Listen up," Ms. Parker says to everyone. "There's a lot of us here, and you'll need to pay attention. Today we are going to talk about dynamics, when we vary the volume of sound. 'Piano' means 'quiet.' 'Forte' means 'loud.'"

She explains that "A Song of Peace" is piano at the beginning. I like piano. We blow like we are whispering through our mouthpieces, and the singers sing quietly too.

Then Ms. Parker signals with her hands for us to get louder, and all the fifth graders on all the instruments play forte so loudly, my ears hurt.

This is how it will be onstage during the holiday concert. I do the math. *Twenty fifth graders in the other class plus twenty-one in Mr. Fabian's equals forty-one.* That is too many too close to play forte. I can't play loud on purpose.

"Once more, and not quite so loud," Ms. Parker directs, looking quickly at me. I hope everyone listens to her.

We play the piece again, piano to forte. It is quieter when we're supposed to be. During the loud parts, my shoulders tense and I concentrate on my breath, counting the beats. After the last note is played, there is a quietness, when the sounds fade, a moment I want to stay in forever.

Madge breaks the silence. "Ta-da! I can't wait for the applause."

"Good job!" Ms. Parker is pleased. "Now each group will perform alone. No talking when you're not playing. Be respectful and listen."

What if the clapping is too thunderous for my ears? I keep thinking about it as fourteen singers sing "Let It Snow," raising their hands at the end like snowflakes. The flutes play their song, "Ode to Joy." Then eleven trumpets do "The Dreidel Song." My hands hover around my ears, in case it's too much, but when everybody plays just right, the sound is nice. Then it's our turn to play "Jingle Bell Boogie."

"Lift your bells—don't point them down," Ms. Parker reminds the trombone players once more.

Next to me, Madge is tapping and blowing.

Everyone's eyes focus on her star performance. The subway girl didn't mind when people watched. Madge is the same.

My insides jump around when I imagine playing in front of a crowd.

"You sound great," I whisper to Madge. And her wide smile makes me feel a little less worried.

At the end of the day, Mr. Fabian gives us a little extra homework to do over the Thanksgiving holiday. Ms. Parker makes us promise to keep practicing. It's as if they think we'll forget everything we have learned so far.

Walking home alone, I hear music in my boots: *step, step, and step-and-step.* Each measure has four beats, four quarter notes equals one whole. We hold whole notes twice as long as halves. I count *one, two, three-and four-and.* I feel the rhythm in my walking, a regular pattern like subway station tile, like a pulse between my ears.

Ms. Parker thinks I can do the concert without earmuffs, and I did okay today. But can I really play un-muffed in front of all the parents, brothers, sisters, and grandparents?

CHAPTER 16

Tonight we're doing a just-our-family Thanksgiving. We've always done it that way, for as long as I can remember. I'm making a turkey handprint centerpiece for our table when Dad comes out of the kitchen.

"Let's go," he says. "We need a few things from Scuto's."

"Do I have to come?"

"Yes," he says. "Let's give Mom a chance to blast some music while she's making a pie."

I'll do anything for pie. I put on my coat and reach for my earmuffs—and stop. Maybe I can make adjustments too, the way Mom does for us. "Maybe I'll go without them," I say.

Dad smiles. "If you want, we can do this, together."

I take a deep breath and nod, tucking my hand into my coat pocket.

Walking to the store, we fall into a comfortable silence. We are listening. There's a siren, a taxi horn, music from a window, and a bird chirping.

Dad stops before he opens the door to Scuto's. "Let's split up so we can be done faster. I'll get the spinach and the bread rolls," he says. "Can you get the apples and cranberries?"

"Okay," I say, but my feet don't budge. A worm of worry wiggles in my head. I thought I could shop without earmuffs, and now I'm not so sure.

"You can do this." Dad places a hand on my shoulder and opens the door with the other. We both take a deep breath as the noise hits us.

He hands me a basket, pointing me toward the produce section. "Remember to focus on one thing at a time. Think of the fruit like birds—apples are pigeons, cranberries are chickadees."

I giggle. "Four pigeons or five?"

"Four should be plenty. Red ones. And get two scoopfuls of those chickadees."

Dad heads off one way and I'm down the aisle

looking for apples. I find the McIntosh bin. I pick up one, two, three, four and put them in my basket.

What's next? Someone is talking about how many lemons for roasting chicken—and I remember chickadees. Cranberries.

I head over to the bulk area, get a bag. I find the cranberries. One, two scoops, and I knot the bag.

I'm doing it!

Someone steps right up to the bulk container next to me. I step back to create more space. I move my feet forward, counting my steps until I find Dad at the checkout registers.

"How are you?" the cashier says, as the scanner *beep, beep, beep*s. I count one, two, three, four apples as she places them on the scale.

"Wonderful," Dad says. "We're having a quiet Thanksgiving."

"Good for you," she says. "Sometimes that's the best kind."

It always is, I think.

Outside, Dad and I exhale into the cool night air. He hands me one bag to carry. "That wasn't too bad, was it?"

"It was okay," I say as we start walking. And I

realize it was. Even if I can shop at Scuto's without earmuffs, I like shopping with them better. But now I know I can, if I have to.

Our table holds more food than ever—and I eat too much turkey and stuffing and sweet potatoes.

"Let's say what we're grateful for," Mom says as she brings out the pie. "You start, Amelia."

"I'm grateful for pie! And good sounds," I add, thinking of the list I began with Mr. Skerritt. "I like trombones in tune. I like sharing candy at lunch. And I like the sound of checkers with Dad."

"Me too." Dad smiles at me. "And I like birds singing in Boston Common with my family."

"I love hearing my daughter play trombone," Mom says.

The list of good sounds fills me up as much as pumpkin pie.

"I was thinking," Mom says as we begin to clear the table. "What about if we invite Deb and her parents over after the holiday concert for a little celebration?"

"Mom," I say. "I don't play flute anymore."

"I know, I know." She stacks our plates. "It would be a gathering with our neighbors, with our *friends*. Maybe we can include Madge and Oma, too."

"I don't like parties," I remind Mom.

Dad looks over at me. "When is the concert again?" he asks.

"Next week," I say.

"You ready?" Dad asks. "Play something for us."

I know he is changing the topic on purpose, and I'm glad to go along with it. So I give them a preview in the living room. First I cover Finway's bowl with his night cloth to protect him from sound waves. I rub the mouthpiece and bring it to my lips. I play "Jingle Bell Boogie" without stopping. Next I play "A Song of Peace."

Mom claps softly. Dad grins. "You've got it!"

"Will you wear your earmuffs during the concert?" Mom asks.

Dad frowns. "I don't see why you need to bring that up—"

"I didn't wear them during rehearsal the other day," I interrupt. "Ms. Parker taught us about dynamics."

"That's great," Mom says.

"The performance will be perfect," Dad says.

That's when I decide. "In fact, I'll clean my earmuffs tonight," I announce.

Mom starts, "But if you're not wearing them—"

Dad rests a hand on Mom's shoulder, and she doesn't finish her sentence. "Good idea," he says.

In the bathroom, I plug up the sink and turn on the warm water. I squirt in a little soap and swish the water as the sink fills. I gently submerge my earmuffs.

I rub the soft fur flaps, washing away playground dirt and city grit. The first day of school seems so long ago. These earmuffs have saved me from screechy subway brakes, piercing flutes, gross Noah sounds, trick or treat yells, wishy-washy Deb, and mean Kiki.

I hold them up. The muffs are as purple as eggplant, and the white band is clean again. I place them on the radiator to dry overnight. Even if Ms. Parker thinks I can do the concert without earmuffs, I'll keep them nearby just in case. I'll wear them when I want to. When I need to.

CHAPTER 17

Everyone is in the music room, putting together instruments, getting ready for the holiday concert. My hands are sweaty as I twist together my trombone. Ms. Parker has thrown open the big double doors, and I look into the gym, where we will perform. Blue-and-green paper chains hang from the basketball hoops to the lights all across the ceiling. The stage has risers for the choir and chairs for us to sit in when it's our turn to play. Teachers shush everyone, but no one pays attention. Parents drop off sweets at the tables lining one wall. Chairs scrape as too many people find seats, say hello, and take off their coats.

Will I be able to play without earmuffs? I finger the

fluff around my neck. And then it's time to line up.

"Okay, smile, everyone!" Ms. Parker says. "Let's go."

We parade behind her to a row reserved for us in the audience, and the choir heads straight to the risers to sing first. Everyone starts clapping. The rest of us sit with our flutes, trumpets, and trombones, waiting for our turn on the stage.

The trombones are going last, which means I have to make it through everyone else. My cold hands grip my instrument between my legs. My earmuffs are off but right under my chair. My black velvet dress is itchy on the inside. Madge wears a vest and looks even more like a real musician than she did at Halloween. I scan the audience until I see Mom and Dad near the back. I give a small wave and try to get into my Melba zone.

Ms. Parker raises her arms, and like magic, everyone quiets. The choir begins "Let It Snow," and I concentrate on Jax's big *O* mouth with smiling edges instead of the many voices singing. The clapping at the end is deafening, easily an eight out of ten, and I sink lower in my chair.

Everyone rustles coats and programs while the flute players thump up onto the stage, passing the singers as they find their chairs in the audience. Like Ms. Parker, I wait for the gym to quiet down. After the last cough, she lifts her hands, her hair flying as she directs. Every note of "Ode to Joy" pierces my ears. They are forgetting the dynamics Ms. Parker taught us in rehearsal. It's all forte. I press one ear against a shoulder, and my free hand covers the other ear. When the flutes stop, the sliver of silence is sucked away by loud applause and more shuffling.

I long to plug everything with my mute. I glance down at my earmuffs. I shift my trombone, shoving one hand under my leg so I won't reach for them. *Eight, nine, ten,* I count the flute players as they return to their seats in the audience.

Ms. Parker calls the trumpeters to the stage. My shoulders are as high as my ears as the forte sound of *dreidel, dreidel, dreidel* marches into my head. The clapping is even louder than the music—I clamp my legs around my instrument so that I can cover my ears.

When it's time for the trombones, my hand is sweaty on the slide as I walk up and sit next to Madge. I waver on the first note but then make it through "Jingle Bell Boogie," counting the beats. The clapping is for us this time.

"Awesome," Madge whispers.

I think so too. I'm surprised to find a smile on my face.

It is time for "A Song of Peace," and Ms. Parker invites the whole fifth grade to stand up and come onstage. There's a terrible scraping of chairs and shuffling of shoes. We practiced this, but I am sweaty and the chairs are not in the same position as in rehearsal. Madge and I have to scoot too far over. We are all so close together, like a packed subway car.

It's all wrong. Where will my slide go on the low notes?

Ms. Parker puts on a cheerful face and strokes the air with her baton to signal for us to play. We begin on F, repeating, and then it goes fast to G, and I stretch my arm down like Melba, the famous trombonist—and my slide s L I D E s all the way down and off, and clatters onto the floor, *clang-bang-jangle-crash.*

My face is on fire. "A Song of Peace" falters. Someone snort-laughs, a sour note squawks, and eyes turn toward me. The song starts up again. Shaking, I slink down, get my slide, and slither off the side of the stage and hide behind the riser legs.

After the last note, too many people are sharp-clapping. Forty fifth graders—minus me—stand, bow, and bang-jump off the risers. I peek around. I can't face Mom and Dad. No matter what she said the other day, I know Mom will be disappointed. Dad will try to make me look on the bright side.

There is no bright side. I am the worst trombone player ever.

Mom is searching for me, her face quiet and concerned. Does she understand? If Mom hugs me like the day in Boston Common, I will cry. I cannot cry.

I grab my earmuffs from under my chair and jam them on. But they don't make me invisible. I need a safe space, a place to tuck into. Paper tablecloths hang over the tables jammed with cookies, brownies, cupcakes, and little cups of red juice. I drop underneath one table, out of sight.

Dad is looking for me too. "Where's my Amelia Mouse?" he calls over the crowd.

Please, please, let no one hear him call me a mouse.

"Squeak, squeak," Deb-and-Kiki say.

Too late.

Kiki says, "Who knew Amelia the mouse could be so loud!"

"She ruined the concert," Noah complains.

I have to get out of here. My ears roaring, I dart out the other side of the table and scurry through the double doors back to Ms. Parker's music room.

No one is there, but the room still feels too big, too open to the gym—I need to hide, and I am inside the instrument closet so fast, without thinking, shutting the door behind me.

I exhale. It's a cocoon, like my tube tunnel. The air is musty. I breathe in Vaseline and brass and rusty snaps holding hard cases closed. I sit against the back wall. I close my eyes, pull my knees inside my dress.

Tears leak down my cheeks. Maybe I *am* a mouse, holed up. The closed door shields me from the sounds of people talking, feet clomping. It doesn't muffle the memory of my slide, my crashing, clanging, slippery slide.

I wipe my face, open my eyes. I just want to go home. How long have I been in the instrument closet? Is anyone looking for me? Maybe even Mom and Dad are too embarrassed to be seen with me.

I stand and turn the knob. It doesn't click. It stops short—

I jerk it back and forth, harder, faster.

Nothing happens. I am locked in!

I knock on the door softly. *Tap-tap-tap.* Then a little harder. *Rap-rap-rap.*

I take my earmuffs off and lean my head against the door. It is nearly quiet. What if the party is over and people are leaving, stacking up the chairs? My knocking won't be able to compete with cleaning-up noises.

My heart runs like sixteenth notes. I don't want to spend the night here in this dark closet against the hard cases. I should yell. I should use my loudest, strongest voice—

I clutch my head in my hands. It's hot—so stuffy. How long before I breathe up all the oxygen? I swallow hard. My tongue is dry. I slump back down onto the floor.

New tears slide from my eyes. Even in an emergency, I can't turn up the volume. I will be known as the mouse who died in the closet for fear of making a sound. I muffle my sobs with my hands.

Suddenly noisy voices and feet break through to my ears. I gulp air and listen. Everyone must be in the music room, packing up!

"Ms. Parker, you didn't leave the instrument closet unlocked," someone shouts.

"The keys are on my desk," she says. "Madge, can you—"

Then I hear a welcome sound: a clinking key, a sharp *click*.

The doorknob twists, and I jump up and trip, falling into a shelf. I scrabble for something to hold on to as the door swings open, and I tumble out, a mountain of instrument cases cascading all around me.

Madge—keys in one hand, trombone in the other—stands still, shocked into silence. Everyone stares.

This is much, much worse than being locked inside.

"Kaboom!" Noah yells into the empty sound, like fireworks going off.

"What happened?" Ms. Parker calls out.

"Whoops!" Madge turns and hollers, so that everyone looks at her. "I didn't mean to knock the cases over! I'll clean this all up, Ms. Parker!"

I lift my eyes in time to see Madge wink. I stand up as fast as I can, wipe my face, brush off my dress. I pick up a case and work with Madge, putting everything back neatly. Madge slides the cases easily onto the top shelf, where I can't reach.

"It's handy being tall," she says. "Long arms." She

holds them out, and I see that her arms are longer than mine, the kind that can slide down for low E without trouble.

"Good trombone arms," I say. I can't believe Madge is covering for me. And not mentioning my slide fail.

Madge closes the closet door. "You okay?"

I nod. "Thanks." I am so glad to be on the other side of the instrument closet door. "You saved me."

Madge flashes her big sunshine smile, which makes me almost forget everything. "It's nothing," she says. "See you Monday?"

"Sure," I say, and turn to find Mom and Dad. I'm ready to go home.

"Where were you? We were worried," Dad says as we start down the street.

I crush my earmuffs on. Mom and Dad are on either side of me. They are sticking extra close, too close. I am almost as trapped as I was in the instrument closet.

"It doesn't matter," I mumble. "I ruined the concert. Noah said so."

"The concert was great," Mom says. "The trombones were the best."

"Mom." I glare. "I made a terrible mistake.

Everybody saw." I'm going to disappoint Madge. I will never go to school again. Or play trombone.

"Everyone makes mistakes sometimes," Mom says. "After a day or two, people will forget."

"It happens," Dad adds. "And the rest was perfect."

We walk another five sidewalk lines. I hear what they are saying, but the words get lost amid the sounds of wheels on the street, bare branches rubbing against each other, and the tramping of boots.

Mom stops at the intersection near Scuto's. "You know, I think this moment calls for a pistachio gelato."

"Or a blackberry-lemon gelato," Dad says. He looks at me slyly.

I sigh. "Chocolate chip."

"I'll go in," Mom says, without pressuring me or Dad to go with her.

Dad and I lean against the market window. I'm still mad that he called me my only-at-home nickname in public.

"That was horrible," I say. "No one will ever forget my mistake." *Or Amelia Mouse,* I think.

Dad's hands are in his pockets. "All I heard was my daughter playing music."

"Making noise on purpose, you mean."

"Beautiful noise," Dad teases.

I snort.

Mom comes out with three gelatos. "Here's to Amelia, our trombonist. You see, if you try harder, it will get easier and easier."

The gelato sticks a little on my tongue as we walk the last blocks to home. Mom still thinks I'm not trying hard enough. And Dad doesn't have to go to school. Gelato isn't a big enough Band-Aid to cover up how bruised I'm going to be Monday.

CHAPTER 18

I think I am sick," I tell Mom.

She hands me my lunch anyway. "It will blow over," she says.

I don't believe her. "I can't go to school today," I tell Dad as he opens our apartment door.

"Don't forget your backpack," he says.

My shoulders drag under heavy straps. The sun is bright, the air cold. I squeeze my earmuffs on tight. I look up and down the street to make sure Deb and Jax are already gone.

Step, step, step down the street. I walk slowly as buses rumble by, cars and taxis race for lane space. *Eighty, eighty-one, eighty-two sidewalk lines.*

By line ninety, I am wondering if Madge will be

my friend again today. The weekend gave me time to multiply my worries. Will Ms. Parker yell at me in front of the whole class? And please, will everyone forget my only-from-Dad nickname?

"Squeak, squeak," Noah says as soon as I walk into Mr. Fabian's classroom.

"Squeak!" Tyler says.

My face is instantly hot. I don't look at them. I am saved by Mr. Fabian, who starts class right away. I bury myself in math and social studies worksheets and backward writing—*sffumrae, sffumrae*—as if earmuffs protect me.

When it's time for music class, my feet feel like they are loaded down by bricks. I don't think I can face Ms. Parker.

When I walk in, I realize that everyone is here— not just the trombonists. Mrs. Spitz, Mr. Tingle, Ms. Min, and Ms. Parker are pouring juice into little cups.

"Congratulations, fifth graders!" Ms. Parker is smiling. "We're celebrating our holiday concert today! We're so lucky that Kiki's mom brought in cupcakes for everyone."

Kiki helps bring out the treats, like she's in

charge. She and Deb are the first ones to pick out a cupcake with chocolate or pink frosting. Forty hands rush the table. I hang back.

"There's plenty for everyone," Mr. Tingle calls.

"Go ahead, Amelia," Ms. Parker says. "Which kind do you want?"

"I'm not hungry," I say. Which is true. My stomach is all tangled.

Ms. Parker crouches next to me. "Are you worried about something?"

"Aren't you mad at me?" I manage to croak out.

"Oh, Amelia, of course not! You did a great job in the concert. You played all the right notes. You even did it without earmuffs!"

I look at the floor. "But I dropped my slide."

"Do you know how many trombonists that happens to? Especially when your slide is well greased."

Ms. Parker's voice is gentle. I lift my eyes. "Really?"

She smiles. "Now you will know how to reach those end notes without extending too far next time."

Madge comes over and hands me a chocolate cupcake. "Here."

"That's so nice of you, Madge," Ms. Parker says, and leaves us alone.

"Thanks," I say to Madge. The first bite is sweet and not bitter at all.

At lunchtime, I walk toward the cafeteria.

"Do you hear that? Oh, it's just Amelia's squeaky shoes," Kiki says. Emma and Lina and Cassie and Deb-and-Kiki giggle.

I stop, clutching my brown lunch bag. Words jostle in my mouth but don't come out. Why didn't I plan a comeback?

Madge comes from behind and loops her arm through mine, and relief rushes in. Nothing needs to be said as we walk together to her table. Earmuffs don't block the squeak-teasing, but the sound rolls off me now.

"Thank you," I say quietly once we're sitting.

I'm not sure Madge hears. She is unwrapping a bursting sandwich of salami, lettuce, and mustard. "You know two-part harmony?" she asks. "That's us. Soprano and alto."

I think for a moment. "Am I the squeaky soprano?" I ask.

"No. We'll blend—I'll be the melody, and you follow."

"Sounds good." I open my lunch bag.

"Ha! *Sounds.* Get it?" Madge laughs, and I manage a smile.

Noah and Jax land at the table with a thump, which makes me flinch. They both say hi like we're all friends, but I remember Noah's squeak joke when he first saw me.

"Here." Noah breaks his chocolate bar and gives me half.

"Thanks," I say. This time I accept. Madge was right—a shared snack can be an apology.

After lunch, we head to the playground. Instead of curling in my tube tunnel, I choose a swing next to Madge. And even though the icy wind blows in our faces, I pump my legs to swing high, like Madge. And then Noah and Jax and Tyler want to play tag, and when Madge is it, she chases me, shoelace charms *clink-plink*ing the whole time, which doesn't bother me as much today.

Mr. Fabian picks Madge and me to pass out worksheets. We use the same-color paper for our collages. We test each other on spelling words. And when the bell rings, I am surprised the day is over.

If I follow Madge's lead, maybe two opposites can get along.

. . .

The next morning, as I'm putting on my coat and earmuffs, Mom gets a phone call.

"Yes?" She looks over at me. "Let me ask." She puts the phone against her shirt. "Madge wants to walk to school with you. Do you want to?"

I nod. Maybe Madge and I are friends for good. Mom gets the directions, and I pick up my trombone case and go right around the corner and up two blocks instead of straight.

Madge is waiting at the intersection, red mitten waving, trombone case at her feet. "Oma is glad I have someone to walk with," she says as we start for school.

Her street is less busy than mine. Fewer cars roar by, and it's easier to focus on conversation. I hear our two pairs of feet, stepping together, like a two-part rhythm.

Madge and I swing our trombone cases front and back, synchronized. We stop and wait for a light to change.

"This is better." She grins. "You walk faster than Oma."

And it *is* better—better than counting sidewalk lines alone or trailing behind Jax and Deb.

• • •

After silent reading, Mr. Fabian hands back the math quiz. Madge mashes hers into a ball. She throws it toward the trash can. It misses.

"You're no Mookie Betts!" Jax hoots.

"No throwing paper, Madge!" Mr. Fabian says.

She goes over and picks it up. "I'll never get division," she complains.

"We take quizzes to see what we need to study," he says. He hands out new worksheets. "Find a partner, everyone."

This time, Madge turns her chair my way. "You may not want to work with me. I can't even remember my times table," she warns.

"You remember notes," I say.

She snorts. "That's different! That's music."

I think of another math trick. "Put your hands up," I tell Madge, and pull her palms together side by side. "Nine times three." I push her third finger down on her left hand. "Look at the fingers up—two on one side, seven on the other. That's two and seven, twenty-seven."

"That's the answer? Nine times three is twenty-seven?"

I nod.

She smiles. "Maybe I can get this."

"It takes practice," I say.

She laughs. "That's what Ms. Parker always says."

Numbers are easier than notes, for me. But maybe multiplication is as much a puzzle to Madge as slide positions are to me. "Can you help me with trombone?" I ask.

Madge laughs. "Math for music? Music for math? Deal."

And we shake hands and decide to practice together after school.

This time, after the bell rings at the end of the day, I am not standing outside alone. Madge and I say good-bye to Noah and Jax.

Jax looks at me. "You walking home?"

"She's coming with me." Madge takes my arm. "We're going to practice."

"Can I come too?"

"You're not a trombonist," Madge says. "You don't even have to practice, since you're in choir."

"Yes, I do!" Jax walks off, singing "A Song of Peace" extra loud, which makes Madge laugh.

We walk side by side, me with my earmuffs on. Madge sings too, until we can no longer hear Jax. She notices I am not singing.

I think of something to say. "Did I ever tell you about two female trombone players I met?"

"Two?" Madge's eyes brighten. "Where?"

"Well, I didn't exactly meet both of them," I say. "One lived a long time ago, and I read about her at the library. Her name was Melba, and she was the first woman to play trombone with men."

"Girls are cool!" Madge declares. And we high-five with mittens on, which is quieter and nice.

"The other one I did see in real life, in the subway station," I continue. She would be surprised to know I play trombone now *and* practice with a friend.

"I'd like to take the T someday by myself," Madge says.

"Maybe you can come with me," I say.

"Maybe." But she doesn't sound convinced.

Madge pulls out a key. We're at her building, which is all concrete and small windows. She and Oma live on the first floor. Inside, the kitchen is warm, and I slide my earmuffs down cautiously. Stew simmers on the stove, and the TV is on.

"Hello, hello," Oma greets us. I call Dad to tell him I am at Madge's. Oma serves us homemade bread with butter. While I eat, Madge and her grandmother talk loudly about the day. I scrunch my shoulders up a bit.

"We could chatter forever," Oma says. She smiles, wagging her fingers at us. "You two make music, go on."

Now I know where Madge gets her smile. When I mention it to Madge, she grins. "Oma says a smile is a welcome mat for conversation."

We share one music stand. Madge and I glide our slides together, reaching for C, back up for F. Sometimes when I see her pinched face in perfect embouchure, I start to giggle. Smiling is bad for T-bone playing, and so we have to break to laugh, slides on their stops, bells down.

"Okay, okay," says Madge, who keeps us on track. "It takes practice to be good."

"Just like multiplying," I say.

"One, two, and three and four," Madge counts, which makes us giggle more.

But then we get serious. We lift our horns, purse our lips, and blow until we play a new song, "Rondeau," perfectly.

Our trombones are in tune, just like us.

CHAPTER 19

Madge and I arrive at school together, pushing open the doors with our left hands, trombones in our right. When we hang our coats in our cubbies, Madge laughs. "Look, we're both wearing blue shirts today!"

Noah shouts, "Twins!"

I look down. Mine is sea blue, almost green. Madge is wearing blue-jean blue with buttons. I say, "Almost."

"Close enough," Madge says, and drops into her chair, making it creak.

I ease into my chair next to her, proud that I don't make a sound doing it.

Mr. Fabian reads from the social studies textbook, his words blending together in a long yawn: colonialismrevolutionindependencebillofrights.

Jax fidgets, and Deb pretends to pay attention. I draw a trombone, but it's hard to do the curves.

Madge sees my trombone doodle, reaches over, and draws a heart near it. I write backward, and turn my notebook so she can see: *Senobmort era eht tseb.*

"Sen-ob-mort," Madge whispers, sounding it out, then snorts: "Senobmort!"

I giggle and write, *Setulf era rof sdaehria.*

It takes Madge only a moment to figure it out, and her laugh explodes as she whispers too loudly: "Airheads!"

We both crack up, and Jax looks like he wants in on the joke, and Deb-and-Kiki glare at us like we are so weird, but we don't care.

"Quiet now," Mr. Fabian says, but something makes him smile. And then I know. It's probably the first time he's asked me, Amelia, to be quiet. I bet he's making a mental note right now to share with Mr. Skerritt.

In music class, we practice "Rondeau" by Mouret. I don't make any mistakes, the same as Madge.

Ms. Parker asks, "Who knows what 'rondeau' means?"

My hand is up, and I don't wait to be called on. "It's like a round—"

"That repeats a melody." Madge finishes my sentence.

I add, "The melody is ta-dum—"

"Ta-ta-dum," says Madge.

Ms. Parker gives us a sweet look. "You two just made a repeating refrain with your words."

Madge high-fives me, and even though I'm wearing my earmuffs, the clap of our hands against each other makes me quickly shut my eyes.

At lunch, I follow behind Madge's magnetic pull toward her spot with Noah and Jax. She squeezes in between them, and I sit at the table edge. I unwrap my sandwich.

"What were you writing in class?" Jax asks us.

Madge grins. "Flutes are for airheads!"

They laugh, and Noah says, "What are trumpeters, then?"

Madge shouts, "Loudmouths!"

Which makes Jax slap Noah on the back, and Noah punches him in fun, and soon they are wrestling, and Madge shouts "Stop it!" and it's all too much—

I hunch my shoulders and press my hands on my earmuffs.

Madge notices. "What's wrong?" she asks.

"Nothing," I mumble.

"Maybe you still need your big headphones," Jax says.

"I don't," I insist, then wonder if they believe it. Maybe I haven't changed as much as I thought.

After lunch, I follow Madge outside.

"Want to play tag?" she asks.

I shake my head. We watch for a moment, and then she tucks her arm through mine. "Come on," she says, and we head for my tube tunnel.

We climb in, folding into *C*s, Madge squirming to get comfortable, her feet almost touching her head in a full circle.

After a too-short silence Madge says, "It's quiet in here."

"That's why I like it," I say.

Another short moment passes. I wonder if I should think of something else to say. I consider trombones, Finway, libraries, but nothing seems right. Usually I don't talk at all in my tube. Madge exhales, squirms some more.

"Boo!" Noah shouts at the mouth of the tunnel.

Surprised, Madge bangs her head on the plastic. "Ouch!"

I press hands on my muffs. Noah and Jax hang on the ladder and laugh.

This time, Madge doesn't. "Leave us alone—Amelia wants quiet!"

"We can be quiet too," Jax says, and they climb in.

"I don't think you can," Madge says.

Noah teases, "What about you? It's impossible for you!"

I press my hands harder against my muffs. Four people and four voices are too many in the tube tunnel. I slither out the other end.

Madge says, "Fine. We're leaving."

I am walking slowly away when Madge pulls me into a run. "Don't let them tag us!" she says, as if we're playing.

It feels good to run, even though Jax and Noah are not chasing us. We reach the brick wall at the end of the playground. I say, "Do you know there is one tree you can climb?"

"Where?"

I point. Breathing hard, Madge heads straight to the stepping-stone crate. Before I can introduce my pine tree, Madge is on top of the wall, grabbing the branch, and climbing up and up. I follow, carefully finding spots to place my hands and feet until I have to stop.

"You're too high," I say. Madge's branch sags. I look down. "The tree is a refuge, not a lookout."

Madge looks down. "What's a refuge?"

"A place for when you're sad," I say softly.

I don't think Madge hears, because she shouts, "You can see forever!"

I cover my ears. Madge is too high, too loud. A thought bursts from my brain: *Does Madge even know how to be quiet?*

When I wake up on Saturday, I remember it's time for the dreaded birthday party for Deb. Me and all the girls in room twelve does not sound fun.

"Let's get ready for Deb's party!" Mom is excited. She's coming too, because she offered to help Deb's mom. Which makes me look even more like a baby, with my mother tagging along.

The only good thing is that Madge will be there.

Even though I know Deb doesn't love reading, I am giving her a book. Books are always the best present. Mom helps me wrap it in tissue, inside a gift bag we found in the closet.

When it's time to go, I reach for my earmuffs.

"Do you need those?" Mom looks thoughtful. "I know the holiday show was hard. Maybe a birthday party will be easier."

I stop. I haven't gone muff-less that much since the concert. Maybe I could try. How loud could it be? "Can I come back home if it's too much?"

"Sure," Mom says.

I hold on to my gift as we ride the elevator up to Deb's floor together. Sue opens the door. "Come in, come in!"

The apartment is decorated with streamers and a banner that says HAPPY BIRTHDAY in bright letters. It's already crowded. Kiki and Emma and Lina are playing a game on the carpet and squealing.

I hand the gift bag to Deb. "Happy birthday," I say.

"Thanks," she says, and adds it to an overflowing table.

I walk over to the window, feeling as lost as my present in the pile.

The doorbell rings again, and this time it's Madge. "Hi, everyone," she calls. Deb's mother takes her coat. Her shoelace charms *clink*.

"Thank you for inviting me," Madge says to Deb as she gives her another gift bag.

Madge joins me by the window. I've never been so happy to see one more person.

"This is going to be fun!" Madge says. "I love parties."

"I like the cake part," I say. Which is the truth.

Sue claps her hands. "Time for a treasure hunt!" She hands Deb a piece of paper. Everyone crowds around to see, but I stand a few steps away.

"What does it say?" Kiki asks.

"It's written backward." Madge winks at me. "Need an expert?"

But Deb doesn't need my help or Madge's. Deb figures the clue out, and the next, each one leading to somewhere else, hidden in the apartment.

In the end, Deb reaches into a pot in the kitchen and pulls out a fistful of plastic bracelets, which she hands out to everyone. The shouts of "Thanks" and "What color did you get?" make me cover my ears again.

Sue brings out a cake, and everyone sings "Happy Birthday." Too loudly. Madge notices I am whispering the words, and slips her arm through mine. Mom snaps photos of Deb and Sue as Deb blows out the candles. The cake is the best part—it's yummy, and people quiet down, until the only sounds are forks scraping on plates, and smacking lips.

And then it's noisy again as Deb starts opening presents. Everyone pushes in too close. I stand by the window.

Deb opens Kiki's present first, and it's a pretty shirt with tiny blue flowers.

"I love it. Thank you!" Deb says to Kiki.

"Open mine next!" Lina calls out.

Deb takes her time with the wrapping paper, lifting tape. She's probably doing it because her mom wants to be able to reuse it. As Deb slides her finger under the tape, the suspense brings a second of silence, and I'm grateful.

Then Cassie ruins it by shouting, "You're going too slow!"

Deb slides out a box of Legos. "Thank you," she says.

All the sounds build—Mom and Sue stacking plates in the kitchen, the scooting closer of chairs, the scrunching up of paper. I cover my ears again. I don't want to wait until Deb opens my gift.

Madge is cheering on the unwrapping, along with everyone else, when she sees me holding my hands to my ears. She stands next to me. "I bet things are a lot quieter than this at your home."

I nod, and then I have an idea. "Want to come over?"

"Now? Do you think we can leave?" she asks.

"The party is mostly over," I say.

I find Mom in the kitchen, and she says it's fine. I can tell she lets me go because I'm having a friend over for the first time since Halloween.

We say thank you and good-bye to Deb and take the stairs, giggling all the way to my floor.

I unlock the door. "Dad's not home either. So we have the place to ourselves."

The first thing I see are my earmuffs left on the sofa. I reach for them, and stop. I don't need them, so why am I about to put them around my neck? Maybe my earmuffs have become my security blanket.

"Your home is as quiet as a fish tank." Madge walks over to Finway, who swims to the top of his glass world, eager for flakes.

"Just the way I like it." I shake some food into his bowl.

"Hellooo." Madge reaches out to tap the glass.

"Don't," I say. "Tapping scares Finway and stresses him out."

Madge pulls her hand back. "Sorry."

We flop onto the sofa. "Thank you for getting me out of the party," I say.

"It's not as much fun when you know someone had to invite you," Madge says.

We watch Finway nibble, mouth opening in an *O*. Madge copies him and I make a fish face too. Our eyes meet and our puffed-out cheeks make us both burst out laughing.

In the quiet when we stop, I think about who Madge is—loud, tag-playing, trombone-playing Madge. She didn't have to leave the party. But I did. Does she really understand why?

"Sometimes I do feel like a fish," I say.

At first Madge giggles, and then she sees I am serious. "Why?"

"Because I hear everything at once as if I have sensory organs running down my sides, like goldfish." I pause. "When everyone is talking, it feels like drums in my ears."

"Like when Noah was mean and banged on the tube?"

I nod. "The tube tunnel is where I go when I need to recharge with quiet time, like this, in quiet places."

"Maybe you need hearing aids that work backward—making sound quieter instead of louder," she says.

"Like when we write backward!" I say. I grow quiet. "If only it were that easy."

"I don't know many quiet places," Madge admits.

Suddenly I get an idea. "I know a place that is really, really quiet."

"Where?"

"The library! Let's go tomorrow," I say.

"If Oma lets me," Madge says. She doesn't sound sure.

But when Oma comes with Mom to pick up Madge, it's all settled. We can go tomorrow, if Mom walks us to the station.

I can't wait to introduce Madge to the quietest place I know.

CHAPTER 20

Ready?" I ask Mom. I have my mittens and coat on, and my empty backpack to fill with books. In case we see a certain subway musician, I pull a dollar from the bottom of my piggy bank.

"Where are your earmuffs?" Mom looks around our apartment.

"I'm not bringing them," I say. A day dedicated to being quiet is a perfect day to practice going un-muffed, as Mr. Skerritt suggested.

Mom is surprised. "Are you sure?"

"I never need them in the library. You know that."

"What about the subway?" she asks.

"I'll plug my ears for that part," I say.

"You are getting good at knowing what works for you, aren't you?" She holds open the elevator door, and soon we're outside, walking the few blocks to Madge's.

"It's nice you've become friends with Madge," Mom says. "And I'm glad you went to Deb's party. It wasn't so bad, right?"

"That's because Madge was there. She understands me," I say. "She's going to love the library."

Madge's grandmother invites us in. My head swells when Mom tells Oma I am capable, independent. Mom is reassuring, like a mama bird who knows we are ready to fly.

"I promise we'll stick together," I say. I stand a little taller to let Oma know she can trust us. "I want to show Madge how great quiet can be."

"And the T," says Madge.

Oma and Mom exchange looks. I don't care. Madge will understand once we're at the majestic Boston Public Library.

Mom walks us to the station, helps Madge buy a round-trip ticket, and waves good-bye once we're through the turnstiles. Then we wait. Madge can't keep still, her shoes clinking on the platform.

"I was nervous the first time by myself too," I say to Madge. I finger the dollar in my pocket.

The station shakes with the rumbling of a green train, six cars long, approaching. Madge claps and cheers, and I cover my ears until the subway stops.

We find seats, and the T lurches forward. Teenagers stare at their phones, and Madge stares out the window, calling out: "There's the Cleveland Circle ice rink! There's a pond. Look, Amelia—geese!"

Which makes me cover my ears and worry. Madge will have to be less loud when we get there. I try to enjoy the ride the way Madge does, the *clack*ing and *whoosh*ing, the blur of trees, bricks, and fences. The noises and sights come as if we're in rehearsal again, everyone tuning their instruments and no one in sync.

Then we are underground, waiting through the heart-stopping darkness, in the rattling, hurtling subway. It's unbearable, and I am sorry I didn't bring my earmuffs for this part. I stick my fingers into my ears, reminding myself it will be fine, once we're in the library.

"Soon?" Madge has to almost yell.

"Yes!" Fingers still in my ears, I nod at the stop map overhead.

The brakes hiss and scream, metal on metal,

and the train stops. We jump up and out the sliding doors at Copley Station.

As soon as we are through the turnstiles, my heart lifts at the sound I was hoping to hear—jazzy notes, rebounding off the mosaic station walls.

Madge turns to me, excited. "Is that the girl trombone player?"

"Yes!" I point. There she is, case open, back against the wall. "She's the one I told you about. She was playing the last time I came."

Madge grabs me, eyes bright. We stand side by side, watching the musician's slide dance up and down, the brass blowing jazz. The music fills us up, swirling warm and low, pushing away all the other subway noises.

"We play trombone too!" Madge says when the girl finishes.

"Cool. I'm Belle." The girl reaches up to her ear and pops out an earbud.

I stare at her ears, one still plugged, one not. What kind of buds are those? I open my mouth to ask, but Madge says all at once: "How did you get to be so good? Where do you go to school? How often do you practice?"

I worry it's too many questions, but Belle says, "I go to Berklee and practice two hours each day." She gives us a postcard. "Come to my concert."

Madge says we will and hangs on my arm, ready to go.

Quickly I blurt my one question: "Why do you wear those?" I point at her earbud.

Belle shrugs. "Keeps other noises down to a simmer so I can hear my T-bone playing in my head."

I'm so excited, I almost forget the dollar in my pocket. I drop it into her case and say softly, "Thank you."

I lead Madge up the steps of the library, and we go through the revolving door. We step onto the beautiful pink marble. The grand staircase is ahead, with the awe-inspiring lions on either side. I almost want to say "Ta-da," but I know I don't need to. The library speaks for itself.

"That was so cool," Madge says, too loud. "We met a real trombonist!" She grabs my arm again, squeezes too hard.

Madge ignores the lions, the marble. She doesn't notice the chandeliers, the old paintings.

"Stop and look up," I say. Today she needs to follow *my* lead. I touch the lion's paw.

Madge doesn't notice. She is already up the stairs. "It's pretty." Her voice echoes all around.

I press my hands against my ears. "You have to be quiet."

"I know, I know," Madge answers, still too noisy as we walk through to the new building and into the children's section. "Berklee! I wonder where that is and if I can go there someday."

"Can I help you?" says the librarian as soon as we walk in. I am sure it's because our entrance is so noisy.

Madge shows her the postcard. "Where is Berklee?"

I need a little space. I walk down a stack of shelves away from Madge, looking for a fresh spine, a new title, a new world. But I can't concentrate. Madge isn't asking for *Alanna* or *Because of Winn-Dixie* or any of the books I like. Belle was my discovery, the library is a quiet place, and why is Madge so-loud-Madge all the time? I've never needed my earmuffs inside the library before, but now I'd give anything to have them. I take down a few books from the NEW TITLES bookshelf.

I walk back over to tell Madge to come and find a book. She is still talking about music schools, and everyone hears her announce: "Someday I will be a trombonist in the Boston Pops."

"I'm going to have to ask you to use your inside voice," the librarian says sternly.

Madge doesn't seem to hear. I pull my winter coat hood over my ears. I can't believe this is happening.

"Amelia, look!" Madge says when she sees me. "The librarian found me a book about playing in the symphony and another about Berklee!" She makes a slide motion with her arms and blows a fake trombone blat through her lips.

"Shhh," says the librarian.

I stop. Never before have I been *shushed*. I want to disappear into the cocoon chairs. We can't stay. We'll have to cut our trip short.

"Let's go," I say in a raised whisper.

"Already?"

Madge follows my lead—at last—but it's too late. We check out our books at the exit.

On the subway ride home, I keep my nose in one of my new books, about Cimorene, who is dealing with dragons—because I Don't. Want. To. Talk.

Madge doesn't seem to notice. "Too bad Belle wasn't still in the station," she says. "I wanted to ask her more about Berklee. Do you think I am good enough to go there one day? How much do the Boston Pops musicians practice?"

Madge stands up tall and slides her arm down, playing air trombone. *"Buhp-buhp-bahm!"*

People glance over at us. I shrink behind my book cover.

"Could we just read now?" I say in my piano voice, so mad that I can't look at her.

Madge makes her imaginary trombone noise again. *"Bahm-buhp-buhp-bahm!"*

"Aren't you ever quiet?" I ask, in my best forte voice.

"I'm too jazzed to read," Madge says, laughing. "Get it?"

I don't join in.

Madge finally hears my silence and slips into a seat and stares out the window.

The words blur in my book. Who talks in a library? Who doesn't know you are supposed to fade into the subway seat, to never attract attention?

We get off at our stop, still not talking. Madge pauses at the corner where she'll turn to walk down her street. She levels her eyes at mine.

"I know I'm not quiet. And I *don't want* to be quiet all the time," Madge says. "Maybe we shouldn't hang out if you won't let me have fun."

She walks away. Without giving me a chance to speak. And she is right not to wait. I don't have anything to say.

Setting the table, I toss napkins every which way.

"What's wrong?" Dad asks. "The library usually makes you so happy."

"Today was not quiet," I snap. "And do you know some musicians wear special earbuds when they perform?"

Mom and Dad exchange looks. "Is this about the earmuffs?" Dad asks.

"No! I didn't bring my earmuffs on purpose. I was trying. The library is always quiet."

"Except it wasn't," Mom says. Her voice is kind, as if maybe she understands why today was bad.

"Maybe—" Dad starts to speak.

Mom holds up her hand and stops Dad from continuing.

"Amelia," Mom says, "come help me with Finway."

My throat is tight as we work together. I scoop Finway carefully out into a jar with one third of the water he already knows, so he won't be shocked by the temperature change.

"What happened?" Mom asks as we upend the dirty fishbowl water into the sink together.

I scrub out the green algae that clouds his bowl, and then refill the bowl. "Madge wasn't quiet," I whisper. "We were *shushed*."

Mom nods, her hand testing the new water to make sure it's not too cold or too hot. I hold my breath as we slip Finway back into his fresh water. He has to trust that we got the temperature right.

"Friendship is hard." Mom's voice is soft. "Sometimes we have to be patient with each other's differences."

I look up at her. "What do you mean?"

"Well, sometimes I have to remind myself to use my inside voice when I speak with you and Dad," she says. "And sometimes Dad gives me space so I can be loud by myself or with Sue."

I remember the way Mom told that woman in Boston Common that I am fine the way I am. "I told Madge why it's hard for me. She doesn't get it."

Mom takes a moment. "Well, if you expect Madge

to accept your differences, then could you do the same for her?"

"I could try." I lean into Mom as we watch Finway swim in his clean new world. For the first time, I'm glad Mom isn't like a goldfish, like me and Dad. Maybe she's right—maybe earmuffs aren't the answer to everything.

CHAPTER 21

It's Monday, and I'm as cold as the trees outside the classroom window. As I watch, it starts to snow, flakes falling silently onto bare branches. I wonder if the trees miss their leaves—dropped like a friend who turns out not to understand you at all.

My earmuffs are on. I am as alone as I was on the first day of fifth grade.

Eyes shut, I imagine myself back at the library, but it doesn't work this time. Instead of my usual quiet zone, I remember too-loud Madge and *shhh* and *inside voices* from the librarian. I try thinking of Copley Station, overlaid with Belle's sounds.

Madge is humming, and I open my eyes and glance at her. She must be remembering Belle too.

If we were talking, I'd say, *That's Belle's song!* But I keep my mouth shut.

Madge sees me looking at her and says, "I don't care about going together to Belle's concert anymore. Oma says it's too far, and anyway, we heard Belle for free."

I can see she's mad, and I am too, so I don't say anything. Giving her the silent treatment is too easy for me.

Later, in the middle of Mr. Fabian's textbook voice reading about historical monuments in Washington, DC, Jax shouts, "It's snowing harder!"

Everyone perks up, turning to the windows. Snowflakes, heavy and wet, are falling. The grass and the sidewalks are already covered.

"Maybe tomorrow will be a snow day," Madge says to Jax.

"Snowball fight," he says, and they high-five. No one high-fives me.

"Quiet down," Mr. Fabian says, and tries to bring us back to social studies.

I hope we have a snow day too. Snow days mean quiet reading time.

When Mr. Fabian passes back the place values test, my mood lifts when I see *100%* at the top of mine.

"Eighty percent! I only missed four!" Madge exclaims.

"You did wonderfully," Mr. Fabian says.

If we were talking, if my feelings weren't still hurt, I would tell Madge how happy I am that she did well. Instead I say nothing, and she walks out with Jax, boasting about math tricks. Under my earmuffs, I pretend Madge doesn't matter.

Deb-and-Kiki watch me watching Madge and Jax.

"The only reason Madge wanted to be Amelia Mouse's friend was for math help!" Kiki says loudly to Deb.

I go still. Her words pierce through my muffs. Is Kiki right? Did Madge and I only practice trombone together because I taught her math tricks? Did we only go to the BPL together because I helped her take the T? Maybe we were never friends.

Madge and I slide into side-by-side chairs in trombone class. Madge plays the A-flat scale perfectly. We run through "Rondeau." I miss the low note again. I edge my chair a little away.

Ms. Parker says, "Let's do that again from the top. More breath, less brass."

Madge blows loudly as if to complain.

I clap my hands over my muffs. I stand up. "Will we ever use mutes, Ms. Parker?"

"Too noisy for you?" Madge says, laughing. When I don't laugh, her face falls flat like a wrong note.

Mom was wrong. We're too different to be friends.

Fingers tight on my lunch bag on the way to the cafeteria, I hear someone shout, "Amelia!"

I stop and slide my earmuffs down, as if I've been caught. I turn and see Mr. Skerritt. You'd think he would know not to yell my name.

"How is fifth grade going?" His voice wheezes. "Ms. Parker and Mr. Fabian have been sharing good updates with me about your progress."

I breathe in and out before speaking. I can't tell him all the things I am worried about and how I've tried muff-less days and how sometimes it's impossible and sometimes it's better. And how right now everything is awful.

"I'm doing great." I grip my lunch bag harder. I feel terrible for lying.

He looks thoughtfully at the earmuffs around my neck. "Have you added more sounds you like to your list? And do you put those earmuffs aside sometimes?"

I stretch the truth a little. "No new sounds, but I can play trombone without earmuffs." Which makes me think of the holiday concert and my slide fail and the locked closet, and I blink hard to make the memories stop.

"I can hear you are trying." He smiles so widely, his ears grow longer. "Be patient. It takes time to adapt."

I swallow, hard. I didn't expect Mr. Skerritt to understand me better than Madge. I walk into the cafeteria even more miserable.

I can't eat at our table. As I turn away, I see Madge jostle Jax, who then collides into Deb-and-Kiki.

"Hey, watch it," Deb says.

"Yeah, didn't your mom teach you manners?" Kiki sneers. "Oh right. Madge doesn't have a mom."

Madge is fire-red-faced, her fists clenched. Her mouth opens, then shuts. For the first time, Madge doesn't fight back. She turns toward me, and our eyes briefly connect.

I don't know what to say, and anyway, we're not friends anymore. I turn away, as if I didn't hear. Between my muffs, I make excuses: *I'm invisible, the old Amelia. It's easier to be silent, easier to not be brave.*

Outside the cafeteria windows, the snow is falling

faster, thicker. Mr. Fabian is talking to the principal. I catch three words—"blizzard" and "close early?" They step out into the hall.

I'm almost to my old table in the corner when a commotion loud enough to reach my muffed ears makes me look back.

I don't know what happened, but Madge's arms are flailing. Her lunch flies out of her hands, and she lands splat on her butt on the floor. The laughter splashes from table to table around the whole cafeteria.

A snort-laugh escapes from my lips. I clap my hand over my mouth to take it back. Too late.

Madge's eyes laser burn me as she scrambles up from the floor and runs out of the cafeteria.

I sit and turn my flushed face to the corner, my back to the cafeteria. I don't watch Madge leave. I pull out my copy of *Alanna*. I try to read but remember instead how nice it was when Madge didn't laugh at me when Noah made me jump with his trumpet blast, or when I fell out of the instrument closet. I really messed up when I laughed at her. How can I undo a sound I made? I grip the curved pages, bending my book open too far. I reach into my bag for my cold cheese sandwich.

MUFFLED

A folded piece of paper falls onto the table.
Someone snuck a note into my bag before lunch.
I open it and read:

Knaht uoy rof gnipleh em htiw htam! S'tel
pots gnithgif.
Ruoy tseb dneirf, Egdam

Best. Friend. And I've been the worst. My heart
crashes to the floor, like my trombone slide.

CHAPTER 22

M r. Fabian comes into the cafeteria and snaps and claps to get our attention. "Line up! School is closing early. Back to your homerooms to pack up!"

Everyone cheers, and I press my hands on my muffed ears. Then I crumple my lunch bag into a ball and carefully fold Madge's note into my pocket. I have to find Madge to tell her I'm sorry, I didn't mean to laugh. I should have gone over and helped my best friend. Why did I believe mean Kiki?

Everyone walks single file back to the classroom. It's hard for Mom and Dad to leave work early. That means Deb's mom is backup to pick me up on snow days. I wish I could go with Madge to her house, to Oma.

In room twelve, I look for Madge. What I notice first is the absence of a sound—a particular sound. The *clink-clank-plink* of Madge's shoes. Her chair next to mine is empty.

Jax sees and notices too. "Where's Madge?"

"She didn't go out alone in the blizzard, did she?" Deb asks. "I wouldn't."

I look at Madge's cubby. Her trombone is gone.

"Maybe her grandmother already came?" Then I realize: Oma doesn't drive. Madge has to walk, and I am her walking partner. Or I was.

"Did she walk home alone?" Mr. Fabian's face is serious. He picks up the phone to call the office.

Something makes me think she didn't leave. If everyone laughed at me, I'd find a place to be alone, a refuge. Suddenly I know where to look for Madge.

I slip out of the classroom. No one notices a mouse.

The playground is under a blanket of white. I slide my earmuffs down to listen. Every snowflake is separate and falls without a sound. The whole city has gone quiet, snow muffling everything.

Outside is all covered up like hands over ears.

Inside is a voice in me so strong and sure, *Find Madge!*

I lift my legs high in giant steps, and with every landing, my feet sink deep into the wet, heavy snow.

I pass our tube tunnel—it's empty except for snow drifting inside. For a second I want to burrow into this hole, away from all my worries. But I can't. Madge needs me.

I trudge through ever deeper snow toward the wall and the pine tree. I feel like I might disappear. I swipe snow off the top of the crate, step up, and look at our refuge. Something is stuck on a branch— Madge's red mitten!

My eyes fall like a pine cone to the ground, my pulse thudding. There she is, below the tree on the other side of the wall, next to a broken branch.

"Madge!" I say in my piano voice. I climb over the wall and jump down on the other side. I kneel next to her. "Madge?"

Madge is not moving, not talking.

A quiet Madge is very bad.

Snow is still falling from the sky, falling onto Madge's face, and she doesn't brush it off.

I remember the dogs in a book walking in circles to stay alive, walking until they are found—

Madge and I cannot stay here. We cannot stop in the snow. But I must stay with Madge. I poke her. "Madge, get up."

No answer. The only sound I hear is the fast pounding of my heart.

Wait. There is something more I hear. It's my voice, roaring inside me, *Be loud, Amelia! Don't be a mouse!*

"Help!" I cry. "I found Madge! Help!"

It sounds feeble even to my ears. I need to be louder than the muffling snow, loud enough to be heard through the walls of buildings, loud enough to be heard through car windows and bus doors.

And then I see it—Madge's black trombone case, buried.

I grab the handle and lift it out of the wet snow. I fumble with the icy snaps, open the case, and reach for the mouthpiece. It's super cold. I twist the parts together, insert the mouthpiece, and hold the bell high. I purse my lips and close my eyes tight against snowflakes.

I blow, and a squawk comes out.

I warm the mouthpiece with my hands and take a deep breath. *I can do this.* I inhale and blow "Rondeau." As I play, I am Melba, daring anyone to say a girl can't, and I am Belle, my sound boomeranging around

Copley Station. I am the trombone, making music on purpose so that someone will hear, someone will say, *What's that? What's going on?*

I play the rondeau again, and I am Amelia, fifth-grade trombonist, harmony to Madge's melody, a mouse with a megaphone, shouting, *I AM HERE!*

When the song ends, my ears are freezing, but I listen with every part of myself. Nothing. No one comes. Madge makes no movement.

And then—

"Ohhh," Madge moans.

"You're alive," I cry.

She half smiles. She stirs, winces. "I fell out of our sad tree. My leg really hurts."

"I'll get help," I say. "Don't move."

I bring Madge's trombone to my lips again. For my friend, I play a bold blast like a subway horn blowing, *HEAR ME!*

"Who's there?" I hear Ms. Parker call out from the other side of the wall. "Amelia, is that you? I heard your rondeau."

"Yes! Madge is hurt!" I yell.

Ms. Parker peers over the wall, sees Madge on the ground, and pulls out her phone. "Mr. Fabian, I found the girls. Call an ambulance!"

Ms. Parker is over the wall so fast. She takes her coat off and covers up Madge. "Are you okay? Your grandmother is coming."

"I'm sorry we left the playground," I say.

"I'm sorry I climbed the tree," Madge whispers. "My leg really hurts."

"You're going to be all right," Ms. Parker says. "We'll take care of you."

The snow keeps falling as we shiver together. At last we hear the wail of a siren.

I pull my earmuffs back over my ears. I don't need to pretend my ears are cold, even though they are. It's okay to wear earmuffs when sirens are piercing.

The paramedics rush over to Madge just as a car screeches to a stop. Out jump Dad and Madge's Oma.

"What happened?" Dad's voice is louder than I've ever heard. He helps Oma through the snow to where we are under the tree.

"Madge is hurt, but she'll be fine," Ms. Parker says.

Oma is a bundle of wool and worry. "My *Mädgchen!*" Her arms cradle Madge like my mom would, because Oma *is* mother to Madge.

I start shaking, and it's not because of the cold. All the fear and noise and tumult feels like vibrations through my body.

"Amelia, are you okay?" Dad asks, wrapping his arms around me. "When I got the call to pick up Madge's grandmother, I didn't know if both of you were—"

"Amelia's fine!" Ms. Parker takes Madge's trombone from me and expertly puts it away. "In fact, she's a hero. She played a song so loudly that we were able to find them quickly."

"I'm proud of you." Dad hugs me tighter. I can't wait to hug Mom, too.

As the ambulance speeds away, he lifts one muff to say so only I hear, "My Amelia Mouse roared."

CHAPTER 23

R eady, Amelia?" Dad asks.

We're standing in the lobby again, like on the first day of school. I hesitate, looking outside. The street and sidewalks are plowed. My earmuffs are on. I'm holding the flowers we bought for Madge at Scuto's Market and an envelope with a secret inside. I wish I could say I'm ready, but I'm nervous.

"One more thing," Mom says. She hands me a box, smaller than the one that held my earmuffs.

"What's this?" I shift my gaze from Mom to Dad. They are smiling. As if they have a secret too.

"Something a little bit better than counting to help you concentrate," Dad says.

"And better than earmuffs," Mom says. "Open it."

I lift the lid. Inside are earbuds. I can see right away that they are not the regular kind for phone calls or music. A different kind. They are little and black and don't have wires to connect to anything. They are like the ones Belle used in the subway station.

"These are designed to subdue background noise," Mom explains.

"For when sound overwhelms," Dad says.

"After you mentioned Belle wearing them, we did some research and saved up," Mom says. "I realize that you may always need help getting through a noisy situation, but at least these won't be as noticeable as earmuffs."

"They are expensive, so be careful not to lose them," Dad cautions.

I hug both my parents, hard. "Thank you," I whisper into Mom's ear.

I then lower my earmuffs and slip my new earbuds in. They fit perfectly, like toes in shoes. I push open the lobby door, turn, and wave. My parents, arms around each other, wave back.

Even though the air is cold, I keep my earmuffs down around my neck. I walk, one sidewalk line, two lines, three. And then I stop counting and listen.

I hear the sounds on the street—car tires through slush, buses braking and hissing as they lower and open doors, boots striking cement, voices talking on cell phones, radio music from a fast truck.

Through my earbuds, the level of volume is about three bars. Not one, like noise-canceling headphones. Not five, like earmuffs. The sounds I hear are quieter and clear—nothing is lost or fuzzy, only tamped down. Manageable. I put my earmuffs into my pocket.

I hear a bird sing and find it on a branch. "Hello, chickadee," I say. "Nice day, isn't it?"

When I turn onto Madge's street, my stomach flip-flops. Will Madge be happy to see me?

Outside of Madge and Oma's apartment building, I carefully take the earbuds out and put them into their special case in my other pocket.

The door opens, and it's Jax, leaving. We've been eating lunch together the last few days, since I found Madge in the snow. It turns out Jax likes books too.

"Hi," I say. "How is she?"

Jax shrugs. "She'll be happy to have another visitor."

He's holding a copy of *Because of Winn-Dixie*,

which makes me happy. "Do you like it?" I ask.

"It's awesome when she claims the dog in the grocery store," Jax says, and turns to walk home.

I take a deep breath. "Hey!" I call after him. "Want to take the T to the library with me and Madge, when she's better?"

"Sure!" He waves his hand clasping the book in the air. I wave back, grateful I've got someone to talk to until Madge comes back to school.

I ring the bell. Will Madge want to talk to me? We still haven't had a chance to talk about what happened between us. Words press against my mouth—"sorry" and "All my fault. Earmuff-wearing is no excuse for not being nice." I wrote my feelings down on paper in case Madge is too hurt to hear me.

Oma opens the door. Her warm smile and their home's hot-bread smells embrace me as always. It makes me hopeful.

"Look who's here to see you," Oma says to Madge. She puts the flowers in water and sets them on the table between us.

Madge is slouched on the sofa, her healing leg in a cast propped on a pillow. Jax's *Get well soon* and name are scrawled on the cast in big letters.

"Does it hurt?" I say first, without thinking.

"Not as much anymore," Madge says. "Taking medicine helps."

Silence falls between us, and for once, Madge is quiet. As if she is waiting. Waiting to hear what I will say. I clutch my letter in my hands. Have I forever lost my friend?

All my planned words disappear.

"Madge—" I take a big gulp as if I am Finway gasping back in his bowl refreshed with new water. "I love the *clink-clank-plink* of your shoelaces."

Madge is so surprised, she laughs. "You do?" Her laughter is like melting snow.

I nod to show I mean it, and Madge's smile is like sunshine again.

"I am sorry for everything," I blurt. I hand her my letter, and she opens it. Tickets fall out onto her lap, along with my note. She reads aloud, turning the words around:

> *"Egdam,*
> *Nac ew eb sdneirf niaga?*
> *Ruoy tseb dneirf,*
> *Ailema"*

"The tickets are for Belle's concert," I say. "Will you and Oma come?"

Madge shouts, "Yes! And yes!"

I clutch my new earbud box in my pocket, and then relax. I glance over at the music stand. "Can we still practice together?"

Madge asks, "Music?"

"And math," I say.

She grins. "The rondeau is better with two."

"And solving math problems is more fun in pairs."

That night, I slide next to Mom, who is working on her computer.

"Let's find a video of Melba," I say.

Mom types in *trombone player Melba*, and there she is, in the results. We watch a black-and-white video of her playing a tune called "Reverie," soft and slow. Melba moves with her trombone, bell raised.

"'Reverie' means 'daydream,'" Mom says.

The sound *is* dreamy. Melba sways, her eyes closed. "It's like you can see the music in her face," I say.

Mom nods. "She plays so expressively."

"She must have felt alone," I say, "being the first one to play in a band with all men."

"And also brave," Mom says. She gives me a hug that is just right.

In my room, I get ready for bed. On my dresser—next to my favorite books, next to my earmuffs—are my new special right-for-me earbuds. I will wear them for the moments when sounds are too much. Sounds like talking-shouting-clapping on top of forte trumpets-flutes-trombones on top of screeching subways-sneakers-chairs.

My earmuffs will only be for cold days now. My new earbuds will make it easier to tune in to what I love to hear:

1. Footsteps on pink marble
2. Trombone notes
3. Jax singing
4. Madge's laugh
5. My own voice.

AUTHOR'S NOTE

When I was a child, more than two feet of snow fell in Boston during one storm, stopping all traffic for days. I still remember the silence—the startlingly beautiful quality of it. When the snow melted, I was sad that our street once more roared day and night with cars. That blizzard was the seed for Amelia's story. A few years ago, I wondered: What if having a quiet respite from noise was more a necessity than a pleasant preference?

I grew up in a gregarious family of interrupters and critics, which shaped my interactions and expectations for others. When I married into a family of introverts with sound sensitivity, though, I gained a new perspective. Living with a highly sensitive partner means knowing how to avoid overstimulation, allowing them processing time before they answer, accommodating their need for extra physical space, and giving them quiet time alone to recharge. Learning to interrupt less and listen more has been a gift.

AUTHOR'S NOTE

Amelia's story grew as I researched and read about sound sensitivity and the use of noise-canceling headphones. I shared early drafts with therapists and teachers to make sure I was plausibly portraying a highly sensitive child. Any errors are my own; ultimately, *Muffled* is the story of only one child's struggle to figure out when to cover and uncover her ears.

I hope Amelia's story inspires you to accept and respect the different ways we experience the world's sounds—from car horns to trombones—and to truly listen to one another.

RESOURCES AND INFORMATION
ABOUT NOISE SENSITIVITY

Hearing is one of our main senses, yet the level of loudness we can handle without discomfort varies widely. Being sensitive to sound is hard to classify, although it is often linked to a diagnosis, such as an auditory processing disorder, misophonia (sensitivity to certain sounds), or hyperacusis (sensitivity to everyday sounds). About 20 percent of people have a sensory-processing sensitivity, a personality trait that can include a strong reaction to noise. In the 1990s, Dr. Elaine N. Aron identified those who are highly sensitive as people who: process things more deeply than others; are likely to be overstimulated by their environment; have stronger emotional reactions to their experiences, including being more empathetic; and are more likely to perceive subtleties.

Whether or not you experience sound sensitivity, the problem of noise pollution is growing. Studies show that noisy classrooms negatively affect reading comprehension and concentration. Recommended decibel levels to encourage learning are in the 25 to 40 decibel range, and yet ambient noise in some classrooms in urban areas can spike to around 70 decibels. (A power lawn mower is about 100 decibels.)

One way to make noisy places such as schools manageable for sensitive children is to permit the use of noise-canceling headphones or noise-suppression earbuds. Although ear protection provides immediate relief, most doctors and educators recommend against excessive usage because children can become dependent on the headphones and become further isolated. To encourage adaptation, therapists often retrain the brain to make a child feel safe and secure.

If you are interested, you can read more about noise sensitivity in *The Highly Sensitive Child* by Dr. Aron (Harmony Books, 2015) and by searching on PsychologyToday.com. There is also an online resource at AllergictoSound.com, a support network for people living with sensory processing disorder and other diagnoses.

ACKNOWLEDGMENTS

Making a book is like making music—from the first tentative note to a final performance, it takes many hours before it is right. And it takes the support and applause of many people. From the first, *Muffled* was guided by my amazing agent, Andrea Cascardi, who saw its potential when it was in an entirely different form. A big thank-you to my editor, Catherine Laudone, who fell in love with Amelia and enriched her story in countless ways.

Special thanks to Merriam Saunders, LMFT, who read an early version with a clinical eye; to private special education and math teacher Julie Durbin for her keen insights into children with different learning abilities; and to Chandos McEowen, the most big-hearted teacher and parent I know.

I'm grateful to my trombone-playing daughter and voracious reader, Sarah Shepherd, for her guidance and perceptive comments, and to my daughters Maggie and Hewson Shepherd, who are the best backup singers a mom could have. To my husband, John, whose love and unwavering support I could not do without. Lastly, thanks to my parents, Emily and John Gennari, who gave me the gift of independence and, when I was young, let me ride the T to the Boston Public Library by myself.

READING
GROUP
GUIDE

Discussion Questions

1. Describe Amelia, her living situation, and her personality. Discuss the ways that noise bothers her. How has that affected her life? What are solutions that she and her parents have tried? What has helped?

2. What is Madge like? Describe the start and progress of her friendship with Amelia. What do they have in common? How does that help their friendship? What is Madge's living situation? Talk about Oma and how Amelia feels about her.

3. Who is Deb? Explain her past relationship with Amelia. How does Deb act toward Amelia? Why are they no longer close friends? Why does Amelia call her "Deb-and-Kiki"? How does Kiki treat Amelia?

4. How do other students at school, including Jax, act toward Amelia? Describe some of those students, and explain why you think they act this way. How does Amelia feel about school as the book opens? Why does she feel like this?

5. What is the music requirement at Amelia's school, and why does it present a challenge for her? What does she try, and how do those attempts work out for her? Why does she end up with the trombone? Describe Ms. Parker and how she interacts with Amelia.

6. Describe some of the other adults at school, including Mr. Fabian and Mr. Skerritt. How do they try to help Amelia? Find examples of times she thinks they are helpful, and when she thinks they don't understand her. Do you feel understood by the adults in your life? Explain your answer.

7. Who is Belle, and how does Amelia encounter her? What effect does Belle's playing have on Amelia? How does Madge react to Belle? Why does Belle wear earbuds? How does that end up helping Amelia?

8. Describe what happens during Amelia and Madge's visit to the Boston Public Library. Why does it create conflict between them? Relate that incident to Amelia's mom's observation that "'Friendship is hard. . . . Sometimes we have to be patient with each other's differences.'"

9. After Amelia and Madge go to the library, Kiki says, "'The only reason Madge wanted to be Amelia Mouse's friend was for math help!'" How does Amelia react to the remark? Shortly afterward, Madge falls in the cafeteria, and Amelia laughs at her. Why does Amelia laugh? How does Amelia feel when she finds the note in her lunch bag?

10. One day, when things are particularly difficult for her, Amelia says, "Outside, I head straight for my tube tunnel, my footsteps on the ladder a prelude to peace and quiet. *Just five minutes,* I think. That's all I need to recharge by myself in my cocoon." Why is the tunnel important to her? What does she mean by "recharging"? Name other places and times where she recharges. What do you do to recharge?

11. Discuss Amelia's relationship with her father and why he understands her in ways that her mother doesn't. Why does he give her earmuffs? Explain what you learn from Amelia's comment, "I don't know how Dad has trained himself to concentrate only on one birdcall amid all the outside noise."

12. After the concert, Amelia's mom tells her, "'You see, if you try harder, it will get easier and easier.'" In response, Amelia thinks, "Mom still thinks I'm not trying hard enough." What does this show about their relationship? What does Amelia's mom want for her? Do things get better between them over the course of the book? Explain your answers.

13. At the end of chapter ten, Amelia hears her parents arguing about her, and she thinks: "*Two parents plus one is three. Three minus one is two. Two minus one is one.* Me, always alone. I rest one muffed ear on my shoulder. Sometimes I wish I could change how I am." How do her observations make you feel? Why

do you think she responded this way? What would you tell Amelia if you were there with her?

14. One of Amelia's techniques for ignoring noises that bother her is to count. Give examples of when she uses this technique to soothe herself. Why does she like numbers? How does she help Madge in math? Why does Ms. Parker say that math is a "'great skill for a musician'"?

15. Discuss why Amelia loves to read and why she says, "Friends in books are the best." What does she mean when she later observes, "You can't have a conversation about math expressions or state capitals or trombone positions with friends in books"? Explain why the library is so important to her.

16. Review Amelia's list at the beginning of the novel, her two lists in the middle, and her list at the end. How does she use these lists? How do they make her feel? What do the lists have in common, and how are they different?

17. Describe the story's setting, including specific places where Amelia spends time. How might the story change if she lived in a suburb or rural area? What if it were set in a different time period? Consider the author's note about growing noise pollution in your discussion.

Activities

1. Ask students to pay attention to sounds they like over the next twenty-four hours, and then pick ten of their favorites. Make a class list of everyone's sounds. Hold a discussion about similarities and differences in the list, and have students tie it to the theme of similarities and differences in the novel.

2. Now that students are in the habit of listening, have them choose a time and place to listen carefully and list all the sounds they hear. They will then use that list to write a poem about the sounds to share with the class.

3. One way that Amelia and Madge bond is to write notes to each other with the words written backward. Invite students to find a scene between two characters in the novel, and compose notes

written backward for the characters to exchange. Discuss codes as a class, including how they are used and why people enjoy them.

4. As a class, listen to a recording of Melba Liston play her trombone (such as the one found at https://www.youtube.com/watch?v=ojwANp_D_fE). Then have students do some research on her life and return to the group with five facts. If possible, read aloud from the picture book mentioned in the novel, Little Melba and Her Big Trombone by Katheryn Russell-Brown, and discuss it along with the information students gather about Liston.

5. The novel uses vivid figurative language to create images in the reader's mind. For example, "Each noise bounces around the walls of my head like a rubber ball" and "Everyone's gaze is like a hundred headlights." Ask students to find other examples of figurative language in the story, identify what's being compared, and discuss the impact of the images. Have each student take a few of the images and write their own figures of speech that the author could have used instead.

Guide written by Kathleen Odean, a youth librarian for seventeen years who chaired the 2002 Newbery Award Committee. She now gives all-day workshops on new books for children and teens. She tweets at @kathleenodean.

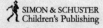

"A bighearted story that's as sweet as it is awesome."

—R. J. Palacio, author of *Wonder*

Meet Ellie, a smart and funny girl with cerebral palsy who is determined to follow her dreams, no matter what challenges life sends her way.

A Kirkus Reviews Best Middle Grade Book

A Bank Street College of Education Best Children's Book of the Year

★ "Ellie is easy to champion, and her story reminds readers that life's burdens are always lighter with friends and family."
—*Publishers Weekly*, starred review

★ "An honest, emotionally rich take on disability, family, and growing up."
—*Kirkus Reviews*, starred review

★ "Ellie takes on life headfirst . . . A feisty, dynamic character surrounded by well-rounded characters just as appealing as she is."
—*Booklist*, starred review

Twelve-year-old Flor faces a bittersweet summer with a pageant, a frenemy, and a hive full of honey.

Honeybees
and
Frenemies

Kristi Wientge